THE BULLY,
THE BULLIED,
and the
BYSTANDER

OTHER BOOKS BY
BARBARA COLOROSO

*kids are worth it!: Giving Your Child
the Gift of Inner Discipline*

*Parenting Through Crisis: Helping Kids
in Times of Loss, Grief, and Change*

Parenting Wit and Wisdom: A Pocketguide

THE BULLY, THE BULLIED, *and the* BYSTANDER

from preschool to high school—
how parents and teachers
can help break the cycle of violence

Barbara Coloroso

Piccadilly Press • London

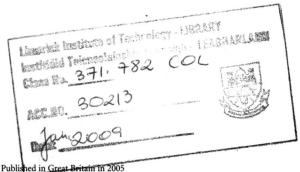
Published in Great Britain in 2005
by Piccadilly Press Ltd
5 Castle Road, London NW1 8PR
www.piccadillypress.co.uk

Published by arrangement with HarperResource, an imprint of HarperCollins Publishers Inc., New York, New York USA

A catalogue record for this book is available from the British Library

ISBN: 1 85340 847 6 (trade paperback)

1 3 5 7 9 10 8 6 4 2

Printed and bound in Great Britain by Bookmarque Ltd
Cover design by Alese Pickering
Cover photograph by Jason Todds
Illustration on page 74 by Joey Coloroso

Papers used by Piccadilly Press are produced from forests grown and managed as a renewable resource, and which conform to the requirements of recognised forestry accreditation schemes.

I think we can't go around measuring our goodness by what we don't do, by what we deny ourselves, what we resist, and who we exclude. I think we've got to measure goodness by what we embrace, what we create, and who we include.

—Père Henri, in the movie *Chocolat*

To David Kent
for asking me to write this book
and trusting that I could.
Thank you.

Contents

Part One:
The Bully, the Bullied,
and the Bystander

Part Two:
Breaking the Cycle of Violence:
Creating Circles of Caring

Preface to the UK Edition

In my recent trips to the UK, I have been struck by the openness and willingness of parents and educators today to confront that which has been a problem for generations and for too long dismissed as "just part of growing up". Bullying is not normal, natural, or necessary and should never be a part of anyone's childhood experiences.

In this book, I've used examples of bullying from all over the world, including the UK. None of our children are immune to the "culture of mean" that allows and supports the bullying that can wreck havoc with their young lives. It is up to us to help our children break this cycle of violence. Children cannot do it alone.

It is easy to point fingers; place blame; fortress our schools; push zero-tolerance plans; mandate a bullying awareness week; stiffen penalties for bullying; or simply ignore the problem and hope it will go away. It is more difficult—and necessary—to create an environment where all children, regardless of their race, religion, gender, physical and mental ability, or their economic status, feel welcomed and accepted in our homes, our schools, and our communities.

A daunting task, but a necessary, and clearly possible, one if we do this together.

BARBARA COLOROSO, *August 2005*

Acknowledgements

My heartfelt thanks to:

David Kent, president of HarperCollins (Canada)—the one who asked me to write the book and trusted that I could—for being there to listen, question and put the energy and resources into making this book possible.

Toni Sciarra, senior editor at HarperCollins (USA) for your keen eye, probing questions, and ability as taskmaster. I am grateful for your patience, support, and friendship through all three of my writing projects.

Iris Tupholme, publisher of HarperCollins (Canada), for your encouragement, support, and willingness to listen to my arguments for early publication in spite of my tardiness with the completed manuscript—and doing whatever it took to make it happen. You are amazing.

Patrick Crean, my literary agent, for listening to me rant about never, ever writing another book and then being there with your wisdom, knowledge, and humour every step of the way through this writing adventure.

Nicole Langlois, for orchestrating the production of the book, bringing together such talented people as copyeditor Sona Vogel, typesetter Roy Nicol, and proofreader Carolyn Black—wow!

Ian Murray, with a deadline looming and me at my wits' end, for your invaluable assistance in cutting through the red tape to finalize the many permission requests.

Martha Watson, director of publicity, Sara James, senior

publicist, and Lisa Zaritzky, publicist, for your creativity and talent for getting the word out and your willingness to create a book tour that was more than a book tour.

Julie Hauck, for giving freely of your time, phenomenal research skills and graphic design talent, but most of all for dialoguing with me as I explored the concept of contempt as it related to bullying. I am grateful for your insight and wisdom.

Satomi Mori Okubo, for keeping our office running and my schedule in some semblance of order this last year, for your insight into the cultural difference between bullying in the United States and your homeland, Japan, but most of all for your friendship.

My friends and colleagues, Linda Ingram, Sally Hauck, Dee Jaehrling, Michael McMannis Derek Okubo, Dianne Reeves, Nancy Samalin, Randy Binstock, and Christine Moore for sharing your stories, your research, your expertise and suggestions.

Barry McCammon, a science educator and author, and Donna Wilson, an educator, counsellor, and family mediator, for reading the entire manuscript from an educational perspective and offering your thoughtful criticisms and suggestions.

The authors I have quoted throughout this book, whose writings have greatly influenced my work.

My three grown children, Anna, Maria, and Joseph, for your love, encouragement, and daily presence through phone calls, e-mails, and quick visits.

Anna and Maria, for once again pitching in to find facts, search for obscure books, and share childhood stories, and for inviting me on journeys away from my desk—even if one of those journeys included rolling a sea kayak.

Joseph, for capturing in your sketches the contempt, pain, and complicity played out in the "bullying circle".

Don, for not only keeping both our home books and our office books in the black while I buried myself in the research for this book, but for laughing, crying, and celebrating with me as we watched our three kids embark on their own journeys away from home.

BARBARA COLOROSO, *July 2002*

Introduction

I shall remember forever and will never forget
Monday: my money was taken.
Tuesday: names called.
Wednesday: my uniform torn.
Thursday: my body pouring with blood.
Friday: it's ended.
Saturday: freedom.

The final diary pages of thirteen-year-old Vijay Singh.
He was found hanging from the banister rail at home
on Sunday.

—Neil Marr and Tim Field,
Bullycide: Death at Playtime—An Exposé
of Child Suicide Caused by Bullying

Bullying is a life-and-death issue that we ignore at our children's peril. It can no longer be minimized and trivialized by adults, taken lightly, brushed off, or denied. Thousands of children go to school every day filled with fear and trepidation; others feign illness to avoid being taunted or attacked on the way to school or in the school yard, hallways, and toilets; still others manage to make themselves sick at school so as to avoid harassment in the locker room. Children who are bullied spend a lot of time thinking up ways to avoid the trauma and have little energy left for learning.

It is not only the bullied child who suffers the consequences of bullying. Many children who bully continue these learned behaviours into adulthood and are at increased risk of bullying their own children, failing at interpersonal relationships, losing jobs, and ending up in jail.

Bystanders are also affected by bullying. These onlookers may observe the bullying, walk away, jump in as accomplices, or actively intervene and help the bullied child. All of these options come at a price.

Breaking the cycle of violence involves more than merely identifying and stopping the bully. It requires that we examine why and how a child becomes a bully or a target of a bully (and sometimes both) as well as the role bystanders play in perpetuating the cycle. A deadly combination is a bully who gets what he wants from his target; a bullied child who is afraid to tell; bystanders who either watch, participate in the bullying, or look away; and adults who discount bullying as teasing, not tormenting; as a necessary part of growing up, not an impediment along the way; as "boys will be boys", not the predatory aggression that it is.

If this triad of relationships is not radically transformed, we have enough incidents in our recent past to convince us that it is not only the bully who may terrorize and haunt our community. Some victims whose cries went unheard, whose pain was ignored, whose oppression went unabated and unrelieved, have struck back with a vengeance and a rage that have racked our communities with incomprehensible horror and sorrow. Others, like Vijay Singh, who reached what they felt was an utterly hopeless and irretrievable point, have turned the violence inward and killed themselves. Feeling they had no other way out of the pain and torture heaped on them by their tormentors, no one to turn to, no way to tell, they made a tragic and final exit:

- January 1999; Manchester, England: Eight-year-old Marie Bentham hanged herself in her bedroom with her skipping rope because she felt she could no longer face the bullies at school. Marie is thought to be Britain's youngest bullycide.
- January 1995; Belfast, Northern Ireland: Maria McGovern overdosed after being bullied. The diary she left behind recorded a life of daily terror at the hands of her schoolmates.
- April 1997; Nanaimo, British Columbia: A grade-four[1] student pulled a knife on another student who was taunting him. According to his mother, the knife-wielding boy had been tormented by his peers for over a year. "He gave up all forms of sport, wouldn't do his homework, and would just end up leaving school—he was angry all the time. He was picked on, period. Home was the only place he could go where he wouldn't get picked on."

  After the knife incident, the boy and his family were required to take an anger management course. The school took no immediate disciplinary steps against the children who had bullied him.
- August 1997; Invercargill, New Zealand: Fifteen-year-old Matt Ruddenklau committed suicide. The coroner's report stated, "Bullying and victimization were a significant factor in the boy's life in the months leading up to his suicide."
- November 14, 1997; Victoria, British Columbia: Fourteen-year-old Reena Virk died after being lured by schoolmates,

---

[1] In grade four, children are usually nine or ten years old. Generally speaking, in the US and Canada, children enter kindergarten at four or five years of age, and they are six years old when they begin grade one.

attacked, and beaten unconscious. Reena's arm, neck, and back were deliberately broken before she was dumped in the Gorge Inlet. She had tried to fit in and had wanted desperately to belong to their group, but she was regularly mocked and taunted about her brown skin and her weight. Particularly startling was the fact that hundreds of students knew about the relentless taunting and even of her death before someone tipped off the police.

Two of the girls who lured Reena to the waterway where she was mobbed and killed were sentenced to a year in custody and another year of probation. The fourteen-year-old said she was angry with Reena because she believed Reena had been spreading rumours about her. The sixteen-year-old was mad at Reena because she believed Reena had been involved with her boyfriend.

• April 20, 1999; Littleton, Colorado: Eric Harris and Dylan Klebold used assault weapons and homemade bombs to lay siege to their high school. The two boys killed twelve classmates and a teacher, injured eighteen other teenagers, and then killed themselves.

Their friends said the two boys were constantly ridiculed and taunted at school. An unfounded accusation was made by an anonymous classmate that Eric and Dylan had brought marijuana to school, prompting a search of their property. Then there was another incident, even more humiliating than the search. "People surrounded them in the commons and squirted ketchup packets all over them, laughing at them, calling them faggots. That happened while teachers watched. They couldn't fight back. They wore the ketchup all day and went home covered with it."

In the suicide note left by Eric, it was apparent that he and Dylan felt bullied and alienated, and in their minds it was "payback time".

- April 1999; Taber, Alberta: A fourteen-year-old boy who was an "at home" student (he did schoolwork at home because he feared school) walked into the main hallway of the high school, shot and killed a seventeen-year-old student, and badly wounded another before surrendering his gun and meekly submitting to arrest. Classmates said he was "everybody's best punching bag". One student said, "He'd sometimes get body-checked into the lockers. They'd try to pick fights with him and he'd just take it. They knew he wouldn't fight back."

  The summer before the shooting, while on an outing with peers, this "new kid in town" was stuck on a rock outcropping, unable to climb up or down. His peers laughed about his predicament and taunted him instead of helping him out.

- March 2000; Surrey, British Columbia: Fourteen-year-old Hamed Nastih leapt to his death from the Patullo Bridge. He left a five-page note for his family describing in detail the bullying and taunting that drove him to suicide: "Mom, I was teased at school by my mates, my classmates, even my own friends laughed at me. They always called me four eyes, big nose, and geek." His mother said one of Hamed's last wishes was for people to stop harassing one another and to realize that taunting is hurtful.

  Hamed's friends felt powerless to stop the taunting. "Everyone gets bullied. But this went too far. We stood up for him, but people couldn't get the hint that this went too far, and this pushed him."

- November 10, 2000; Mission, British Columbia: Fourteen-year-old Dawn Marie Wesley hanged herself with her dog's leash in her bedroom. She left a suicide note naming three girls at her school she said were "killing her" because of their bullying: "If I try to get help it will get worse. They are always looking for a new person to beat up and they are the toughest girls. If I ratted they would get suspended and there would be no stopping them. I love you all so much." The girls named in the note were suspended from school.

- January 2001; Holyoke, Colorado: Fourteen-year-old Miranda Whittaker killed herself with a gun in her family's home. Her parents filed a suit against local school officials for their failure to "deal seriously with the aftermath of the sexual assault" of their daughter. They accused the school district of "failing to provide their daughter with a safe and secure learning environment free of sexual harassment".

  According to the suit, Miranda was a twelve-year-old student when she reported that a sixteen-year-old popular student athlete in this small rural community had raped her. The sixteen-year-old pleaded guilty to second-degree sexual assault and was sentenced to four years of probation and a suspended sentence. (He was later accused of raping and impregnating another girl. Paternity tests concluded he was the father of the child.)

  Miranda's parents alleged that school officials did nothing to stop other students as well as teachers from taunting and harassing their daughter. Miranda was called a "slut" and a "whore", blamed and shamed for being a rape victim of a star student. Her parents also contend that the school took no action against the boy, against whom Miranda had obtained a restraining order. In their lawsuit, the parents said that one teacher (Miranda's basketball coach, who made it clear she supported the boy) forced the girl to stand next to her rapist in class, even though the restraining order required he not be within her sight. School officials denied any wrongdoing.

- March 5, 2001; Santee, California: Charles Andrew Williams, a fifteen-year-old high school freshman, brought a gun to school, shot and killed two schoolmates, and wounded thirteen more as well as several adults.

  Friends said he was picked on constantly. "He was so skinny that some people called him 'Anorexic Andy'." His older brother, Michael, said Andy was used to being taunted. "He has big ears and he's real skinny. People liked to pick on him. It was like that as long as I can remember."

  "He was always getting picked on. He's scrawny, he's little," said a friend, Neil O'Grady. "People think he's dumb. Recently, he had two skateboards stolen." Another teen admitted, "We abused him pretty much, I mean verbally. I called him a skinny faggot one time."

- March 7, 2001; Williamsport, Pennsylvania: Elizabeth Bush, a fourteen-year-old eighth-grader, brought her father's gun to school and shot and wounded a friend who had allegedly turned on her and joined in with her tormentors, who often called her "idiot, stupid, fat, and ugly".

- November 2001; Tokyo, Japan: A primary-school boy

stabbed his tormentor in an attempt to end months of *ijime* (bullying).

- April 8, 2002; Halifax, Nova Scotia: A popular and outgoing student, fourteen-year-old Emmet Fralick shot and killed himself in his bedroom. He left behind a suicide note saying he could no longer take the bullying from his peers. It was reported that Emmet faced extortion, threats, and beatings from other teenagers.

The list could go on for many more pages, detailing incidents from countries around the world. The common thread in all of these accounts is that these children were bullied relentlessly and, in most cases, the bullying went on without substantial objections, indignation, adequate intervention, or outrage. We are devastated by the final act of violence but rarely outraged by the events that led to that final act. The bottom line: These tragic outcomes need not have happened. Bullying is a learned behaviour. If it can be learned, it can be examined, and it can be changed. Whether you're dealing with a long-standing or escalating problem, or whether you're concerned because your child is exhibiting some of the early warning signs—or you've seen behaviours among his or her friends that concern you—this book can help.

> *We cannot live only for ourselves. A thousand fibers connect us with our fellow men; and among those fibers, as sympathetic threads, our actions run as causes, and they come back to us as effects.*

> —Herman Melville

When the dignity and safety of an individual is assaulted, the dignity and fabric of the group as a whole is diminished.

—William M. Bukowski and Lorrie K. Sippola,
"Groups, Individuals, and Victimization:
A View of the Peer System",
Peer Harassment in School

PART ONE

The Bully, the Bullied, and the Bystander

I find myself sometimes curious, often times irritated, and occasionally astonished by the whole concept of bullies, bullied, and those who are witness to the activity and remain silent. That we lack the skills of dealing with bullying in peacefully effective ways screams at us from the news headlines. And there is a line crossed all too often where the bullied becomes the bully. The idea that being excluded, shunned, ridiculed, ostracized, and physically assaulted by the bullying faction merits vengeance and violence is but one of those self-degrading ideas that we embrace, creating a cure that is worse than the disease.

—Dianne Reeves, in a letter to the author

CHAPTER ONE

Three Characters and a Tragedy

All the world's a stage,
And all the men and women merely players.
They have their exits and their entrances,
And one man in his time plays many parts, . . .

—William Shakespeare,
As You Like It, act 2, scene 7

Actor: Someone who behaves in a way intended to deceive or impress others.

Character Actor: Someone who specializes in playing the roles of unusual or distinctive characters.

Typecasting: To give an actor a series of parts of the same type, to the extent that the performer becomes associated with that kind of role and is overlooked for others.

The bully, the bullied, and *the bystander* are three characters in a tragic play performed daily in our homes, schools, playgrounds, and streets. As the examples in the introduction make clear, the play is real and the consequences can be deadly. A child who is playing "the bully" dresses, speaks, and acts the part, as do "the bullied" and "the bystander". It is the posturing, the words, the actions, and the consequences of these elements combined that is the concern of this book. Most young children try out all three roles and play each one with relative ease, then abandon the bully and bullied roles to become bystanders. Some children play both bully and bullied and move effortlessly between the two. A few get typecast and find it almost impossible to break out of the role they have mastered, with no opportunity to develop more constructive social skills.

Typecasting raises the issue of language. As a former teacher, I have seen how easy, efficient, and nonproductive it is to use language as a kind of shorthand to mould a diagnosis and a child into one entity and use that term as if it encapsulates that child's entire identity. A child who has diabetes is identified as a *diabetic*, a child with epilepsy is an *epileptic*, a child with asthma is an *asthmatic*, a child with a learning disability is a *learning-disabled child*. It takes a bit more effort and a few more syllables to say a *child who has epilepsy, a child who has asthma, a child with a learning disability*. I think it is worth both more effort and more syllables to keep from defining a child by his or her illness or disability.

So why use the terms *the bully, the bullied*, and *the bystander*? Some argue that to label the participants of a bullying episode is to typecast them and prevent them from moving out of their negative character roles. These writers prefer to focus on changing behaviour and avoid labelling participants: *the person bullying, the person bullied, the person observing*. The emphasis is on providing alternatives for those taking part in or subjected to bullying.

Others use labels to intentionally typecast kids, viewing the bullying issue in black and white, as a good guy/bad guy script: "Bullies and Their Victims; the Game of Blame and Shame". In this view, it's a matter of them versus us—get rid of the bully and you get rid of the problem.

A third option is to use labels as identifiers of certain roles and the behavioural characteristics of those roles. I choose this option. When any one of these terms—the bully, the bullied, or the bystander—is used in this book, it is intended to identify only a role that a child is performing at that moment, in that one scene of one act in a longer play. It is not intended to define or permanently label a child. The goal is to gain a clearer understanding of these roles and how the interactions involved in such role-playing, though commonplace in our culture, are not healthy, not normal, and certainly not necessary and in fact can be devastating to children playing any of the three characters.

Once we understand these roles, we can begin to rewrite the script and create alternative, healthier roles that require no pretence and no violence. We can rechannel the governing or controlling behaviour of the bully positively into leadership activities. The nonaggressive behaviours of the bullied can be acknowledged and developed as strengths. The role of bystander can be transformed into that of a witness: someone willing to stand up, speak out, and act against injustice.

Our children are not merely acting out their scripts, they are living them. They can't go home after a performance and "get real", because home is a part of their stage. But the scripts can be rewritten, new roles created, the plot changed, the stage reset, and the tragic ending scrapped. The actors can't do it alone. We adults have to get out of our seats—we cannot afford to be a passive, inattentive, bored, alarmed, or deeply saddened audience. We can't walk out, close the show, and send it somewhere else. We can't merely banish the bully and mourn the bullied child. It's the roles that must be abandoned, not our children. Our children need a new play, and we adults can become active participants in a total rewrite. Before we can begin the rewrite, though, we need to analyse and understand the original tragedy.

Scenes from a Tragedy

The Bully, the Bullied, and the Bystander is a play of many versions with the same tragic themes rendered by different actors, wearing different costumes, reading different lines.

The scene is set:

- A culture that rewards bullies and blames targets.
- Schools that pretend not to have a bullying problem, that have a well-established hierarchy of student cliques, and that have no effective policies, procedures, or programmes to address bullying.
- Parents who model and/or teach bullying at home.
- Adults who don't see the suffering or hear the cries of kids who are bullied.

ACT ONE: SURVEY THE LANDSCAPE

The bully surveys the playground, checks out the other characters in an attempt to identify potential targets, and looks to the audience to see if any adult is paying attention.

The bullied is playing with a ball against the schoolhouse wall, unaware that he is being observed by the bully.

The bystanders are throwing balls into the basketball net, laughing, enjoying one another's company.

ACT TWO: TEST RUN

The bully brushes up against his target as if by accident and observes the reaction of both the bullied and the bystanders; uses crude and hurtful names to depersonalize the target.

The bullied reacts with a shrug and slumps down, is uneasy, feels fear in his gut, but doesn't know what to do.

The bystanders either look away or laugh, giving support and tacit approval to the bully. For some, this is a form of entertainment at the target's expense.

ACT THREE: ACTION

The bully shoves the bullied; views this target as an object of ridicule, not as a peer or equal; grabs the ball and flings it across the playground.

The bullied blames himself for being attacked, bullies himself with words ("I'm a klutz, I'm weak, I'm a nobody"), kicks himself for being inadequate, feels powerless against the bully, tries to rationalize that the bully doesn't really mean to hurt him.

Some bystanders move away from the scene and feel guilty for not stopping the bully. They feel helpless and afraid themselves, and they wonder if they will be next. Other bystanders join in, verbally taunt the target, and start kicking the ball among themselves. This process of depersonalization and desensitization enables both the bully and the bystanders to commit more severe acts of violence and aggression against the bullied kid.

ACT FOUR: EMBOLDENED

The bully finds new opportunities to taunt and torment the bullied kid. He becomes more physically aggressive and threatens more harm in order to instil terror in his target. He feels powerful when engaging the target. The results give him a sense of glee and pleasure.

The bullied spends class time figuring out ways to avoid the bully. He can't concentrate on schoolwork; gets physically sick; makes excuses to avoid the playground, toilets, and lunchroom; feels helpless and hopeless.

The bystanders again break into two camps: one group stays clear of the bully to avoid any confrontation; the other group joins in the bullying. Both groups fear the bully and convince themselves that they won't be next by rationalizing that the target had it coming, deserved what he got, was a wimp, was outside their limited circle of caring.

ACT FIVE: PINNACLE OF PAIN

The bully continues to torment and hurt his target with increasing viciousness. He becomes typecast in the role of bully, fails to develop healthy relationships, lacks the ability to take another's perspective, is void of empathy, and views himself as powerful and well liked. His sense of entitlement, his intolerance, and his pleasure in excluding others are the hallmarks of his reputation.

The bullied slumps further into depression and rage—he is

angry with himself, with the bully, with the bystanders, and with the adults who wouldn't or couldn't help him. Because he's been absent a lot and can't concentrate when in school, he does poorly academically—another source of pressure and shame. Not able to come up with constructive ways to regain control of his life, he spends time thinking about ways to get revenge. He might join a group of other "undesirables", who together concoct a plan for revenge, or he might withdraw further into isolation and exile.

Bystanders do one of four things: 1. remain fearful of the bully and continue to blame the target for becoming a victim; 2. join the bullying; or, 3. not seeing anyone else intervening, shrug their shoulders, feeling helpless to stop the bullying or, worse yet, 4. seeing no need to stop it.

ACT SIX: FINALE

The bully grows up with a poor sense of self, stunted social skills, and aggressive responses to provocations, slights, and perceived provocations. His bullying becomes a way of life in his personal, social, and work relationships. Seeing bullying as normal, he minimizes its damaging effects with rationalizations and excuses. He may bully his own children, continuing the cycle of violence. He might move on to criminal activities and end up in jail.

The bullied, not trusting adults to protect or help him and isolated from healthy peer relationships, does whatever it takes to get rid of the pain. The pent-up rage may explode into violent aggression against the bully and all those who appeared to have helped the bully, those who stood by and did nothing, and the adults who failed to protect him. In an alternate scenario, the bullied child, with the rage imploding, kills himself to make the pain stop. In a third variant that combines the other two and is all too familiar today, he goes on a rampage that ends in multiple deaths, then kills himself or effectively ends his life by being put in jail.

Bystanders either get caught in the crossfire, grow up guilt-ridden for not intervening, or become so desensitized to the violence that they minimize and normalize bullying as just part of childhood—not a big deal, just another way to toughen kids up. They pass their assumptions to their children, and the stage is set for a reprise.

Replace "he" with "she"; replace physical bullying with shunning, rumours, and gossip; change the reason the bullied child was seen as a potential target—such as race, gender (including sexual orientation), religion, physical attributes, or mental abilities—and you have a whole new play with the same theme, acts, and tragic ending.

This tragedy has had too long a run.

In the rest of Part One, we'll discuss the three main characters—their makeup, their lines, their actions, their impact on one another, and the cycle of violence they create together, as well as the dangerous myths that help perpetuate this cycle. In Part Two, we'll explore how the home, school, and community can be players in setting the stage for bullying to occur and casting children into their roles. Most important, we'll look at ways for all three to come together to break the cycle of violence and create circles of caring where all children can thrive.

> *We have this thing about finding some simple explanation which gives us the illusion that there are*

simple solutions. . . . When you look at school violence, what elevates risk is a whole bunch of things—violence in the family, violent television, bullying and being bullied, a culture that promotes violence as a successful way of getting what you want. It is most likely that the situation we're in now is an accumulation of all these factors as opposed to any one of them.

—Dr Howard Spivak, professor of pediatrics and community health at Tufts University School of Medicine and author of an editorial accompanying the first large-scale national study on bullying in schools in the US, reported in the April 2000 issue of *Journal of the American Medical Association*

CHAPTER TWO

The Bully

Can we not teach children, even as we protect them from victimization, that for them to become victimizers constitutes the greatest peril of all, specifically the sacrifice—physical and psychological—of the well-being of other people? And that destroying the life or safety of other people, through teasing, bullying, hitting, or otherwise "putting them down," is as destructive to themselves as to their victims.

—Lewis P. Lipsitt,
Child and Adolescent Behavior Letter,
Brown University (May 1995)

Bullies come in all different sizes and shapes: some are big, some are small; some bright and some not so bright; some attractive and some not so attractive; some popular and some absolutely disliked by almost everybody. You can't always identify bullies by what they *look* like, but you can pick them out by what they *act* like. They have their lines and actions down; their roles are often rehearsed at home. Sometimes they take their cue from the movies they see, the games they play, the kids they hang around with, the school they attend, and the culture that surrounds them. To the untrained eye, it may look as if they are only teasing, just pretending, having a good old-fashioned fistfight, or just siblings doing the usual rivalry stuff. They are not. They are involved in serious acting with serious consequences for themselves, the kids they bully, and the community as a whole.

In a study conducted in 2001 by the Kaiser Foundation, a US health care philanthropy organization, in conjunction with the Nickelodeon TV network and Children Now, a youth advocacy group, almost three-quarters of preteens interviewed said bullying is a regular occurrence at school and that it becomes even more pervasive as kids start high school; 86 percent of children between the ages of twelve and fifteen said that they get teased or bullied at school—making bullying more prevalent than smoking, alcohol, drugs, or sex among the same age group. More than half of children between the ages of eight and eleven said that bullying is a "big problem" at school. "It's a big concern on kids' minds. It's something they're dealing with every day," reported Lauren Asher of the Kaiser Foundation.

Dr Debra J. Pepler and her colleagues at the LaMarsh Centre for Research on Violence and Conflict Resolution at York University, Toronto, conducted a descriptive study on bullying at the request of the Toronto Board of Education. Drawing on answers given by the 211 students in fourteen classes from grades four through eight, their teachers, and their parents, two other researchers, S. Zeigler and M. Rosenstein-Manner (1991), compiled the following statistics:

- 35 percent of the kids were directly involved in bullying incidents.
- Bullying peaked in the eleven- to twelve-year-old age group.
- 38 percent of students identified as special education students (students with special needs) were bullied, compared with 18 percent of other students.
- 24 percent reported that race-related bullying occurred now and then or often.
- 23 percent of the students bullied and 71 percent of the teachers reported that teachers intervened often or almost always.

This last statistic coincides with the other data collected about parents and teachers in the survey. Parents and teachers greatly underestimated the frequency of bullying when compared with student responses.

Young children are confronting bullying more than many of us realize or are willing to admit. According to the US National Association of School Psychologists, about one in seven schoolchildren has been either a bully or the target of a bully. Kids, parents, and educators need to feel more comfortable talking together about what's really going on in kids' lives. In order to do that, we need a common language and an understanding of the dynamics of bullying.

Four Markers of Bullying

Bullying is a conscious, wilful, and deliberate hostile activity intended to harm, induce fear through the threat of further aggression, and create terror. Whether it is premeditated or seems to come out of the blue, is obvious or subtle, "in your face" or behind your back, easy to identify or cloaked in the garb of apparent friendship, done by one kid or a group of kids, bullying will always include these three elements.

1. **Imbalance of power**: The bully can be older, bigger, stronger, more verbally adept, higher up on the social ladder, of a different race, or of the opposite sex (more on this one later). Sheer numbers of kids banded together to bully can create this imbalance. Bullying is not sibling rivalry, nor is it fighting that involves two equally matched kids who have a conflict.

2. **Intent to harm**: The bully means to inflict emotional and/or physical pain, expects the action to hurt, and takes pleasure in witnessing the hurt. This is no accident or mistake, no slip of the tongue, no playful teasing, no misplaced foot, no inadvertent exclusion, no "Oops, I didn't mean it".

3. **Threat of further aggression**: Both the bully and the bullied know that the bullying can and probably will occur again. This is not meant to be a one-off event.

When bullying escalates unabated, a fourth element is added:

4. **Terror**: Bullying is systematic violence used to intimidate and maintain dominance. Terror struck in the heart of the child targeted is not only a means to an end, it is an end in itself. This is not a one-off incident of aggression elicited by anger about a specific issue, nor is it an impulsive response to a rebuke.

Once terror is created, the bully can act without fear of recrimination or retaliation. The bullied child is rendered so powerless that he is unlikely to fight back or tell anyone about the bullying. The bully counts on bystanders becoming involved in participating or supporting the bullying or at least doing nothing to stop it. Thus the cycle of violence begins.

The Ways and Means of Bullying

There are three kinds of bullying: verbal, physical, and relational. All three can pack a wallop alone but are often combined to create a more powerful attack. Boys and girls use verbal bullying equally. Boys tend to use physical bullying more often than girls do, and girls use relational bullying more often than boys. This difference has more to do with the socialization of males and females in our culture than with physical prowess or size. Boys tend to play in large, loosely defined groups, held together by common interests. They establish a pecking order that is clearly delineated and honoured. There is jockeying for a dominant position. Physical prowess is honoured above intellectual ability. Thus we see boys shoving smaller, weaker, often smarter boys into lockers, calling them "wimp", "nerd", "sissy" (the latter word both an allusion to the emotional makeup of a boy and reflecting the attitude that girls are on the lowest rung of the ladder of power and respect).

Physical bullying is not exclusive to boys. Bigger girls are known to trip, shove, and poke smaller girls or smaller boys. Girls just have a more powerful tool in their arsenal to use against other girls—relational bullying. Compared with boys, girls tend to play in small, more intimate circles with clearly defined boundaries, making it easier to harm a girl merely by excluding her from a social circle.

VERBAL BULLYING

"Sticks and stones may break my bones, but words will never hurt me" is a lie. Words are powerful tools and can break the spirit of a child who is on the receiving end. Verbal abuse is the most common form of bullying used by both boys and girls. It accounts for 70 percent of reported bullying. It is easy to get away with and can be whispered in the presence of adults and peers without detection. It can be yelled out in the playground and blend into the din heard by the playground supervisor, written off as crass dialogue among peers. It is quick and painless for the bully and can be extremely harmful to the target. Younger children who haven't yet developed a strong sense of self are the most susceptible to it, although repeated attacks can wear down almost any child regardless of age. The list of the verbal taunts to Hamed Nastih, the fourteen-year-old who leapt to his death in Surrey, British Columbia, filled four of the five pages of his suicide note. The most common directed at him were "four eyes", "big nose", "geek", "queer", and "fag".

If verbal bullying is allowed or condoned, it becomes normalized and the target dehumanized. Once a child has been dehumanized, it becomes easier to attack that child without eliciting the normal compassion from those who are within earshot. When a child becomes the regular butt of jokes, he or she is often excluded from other, more prosocial activities, the last to be chosen, the first to be eliminated. Who wants to have a loser on their side?

Verbal bullying can take the form of name-calling, taunting, belittling, cruel criticism, personal defamation, racist slurs, and sexually suggestive or sexually abusive remarks. It can involve extortion of lunch money or possessions, abusive phone calls, intimidating e-mails, anonymous notes containing threats of violence, untruthful accusations, false and malicious rumours, and gossip—yes, gossip can be a form of bullying. Hesiod, an eighth-century BC poet, called gossip "mischievous, light, and easy to raise, but grievous to bear and hard to get rid of". Gossip cheapens human relationships and sensationalizes a bullied child's problems, mistakes, and interactions: "Did you hear what she did?"

Of the three forms, verbal bullying is the one that can stand alone the easiest, is often the entrée to the other two, and can be the first step toward more vicious and degrading violence.

PHYSICAL BULLYING

Although it is the most visible and therefore the most readily identifiable form of bullying, physical bullying accounts for less than one third of the bullying incidents reported by children. It includes slapping, hitting, choking, poking, punching, kicking, biting, pinching, scratching, twisting limbs into painful positions, spitting, and damaging or destroying clothes and property belonging to the bullied child. The older and stronger the bully, the more dangerous this kind of attack becomes, even if *serious* harm is not intended: "I only meant to scare him. I didn't mean to break his arm."

The child who regularly plays this role is often the most troubled of all the bullies and most likely to move on to more serious criminal offences.

RELATIONAL BULLYING

The most difficult to detect from the outside, relational bullying is the systematic diminishment of a bullied child's sense of self through ignoring, isolating, excluding, or shunning. Shunning, an act of omission, joined with rumour, an act of commission, is a forceful bullying tool. Both are unseen and hard to detect. The child being talked about may not even hear the rumour but will still suffer from its effects. ("Stay away from him, he has the lurgy." "Don't hang around with her; she's slept with half the boys on the baseball team. People will think you're just as easy.")

Relational bullying can be used to alienate and reject a peer or to purposefully ruin friendships. It can involve subtle gestures such as aggressive stares, rolling of eyes, sighs, frowns, sneers, sniggers, and hostile body language.

Relational bullying is at its most powerful in the middle years, with the onset of adolescence and the accompanying physical, mental, emotional, and sexual changes. It is a time when young teens are trying to figure out who they are and trying to fit in with their peers. Intentionally excluding a child from sleepovers, birthday parties, and playground games is often overlooked as a form of bullying because it is not as readily identifiable as name-calling or a fist in the face; the results are not as obvious as a black eye or a torn jacket; and the pain it causes is usually hidden or, when expressed, dismissed ("You wouldn't want to go to their party anyway").

The Makeup of a Bully

There are lots of reasons some kids use their abilities and talents to bully other people. No single factor tells the whole story.

Bullies don't come out of the womb as bullies. Inborn temperament is a factor, but so, too, are what social scientist Urie Bronfenbrenner called "environmental influences": children's home life, school life, and the community and culture (including the media) that permit or encourage such behaviour. The one thing we know for sure is that bullies are *taught* to bully.

There are seven kinds of bullies:

1. The *confident bully* doesn't walk onto the scene; he swaggers onto it, throwing his weight around figuratively and literally. He has a big ego (as opposed to a strong one), an inflated sense of self, a sense of entitlement, a penchant for violence, and no empathy for his targets. He feels good only to the degree that he feels a sense of superiority over others. Peers and teachers often admire him because he has a powerful personality. This does not mean that he has a lot of friends. Friendships are based on trust, loyalty, and mutual respect, not typically characteristics of any bully.

2. The *social bully* uses rumour, gossip, verbal taunts, and shunning to systematically isolate her selected targets and effectively exclude them from social activities. She is jealous of others' positive qualities and has a poor sense of self, but she hides her feelings and insecurities in a cloak of exaggerated confidence and charm. Devious and manipulative, she can act as if she is a caring and compassionate person, but it is only a guise to cover for her lack of true empathy and a tool to get what she wants. She may be popular, but she is not someone other kids would want to confide in, lest they, too, become a target for her bullying.

3. The *fully armoured bully* is cool and detached. He shows little emotion and has strong determination to carry out his bullying. He looks for an opportunity to bully when no one will see him or stop him. He is vicious and vindictive toward his target but charming and deceptive in front of others, especially adults. He appears to have what is known as a "flat affect"—that is, a cold and unfeeling demeanour; in reality he has buried his feelings so deep in a place of darkness and growing angst that even he has trouble finding and identifying them.

4. The *hyperactive bully* struggles with schoolwork and has poorly developed social skills. He usually has some kind of learning disability, doesn't process social cues accurately, often reads hostile intent into other kids' innocent actions, reacts aggressively to even slight provocation, and justifies his aggressive response by placing blame outside of himself: "He hit me first." The hyperactive bully has trouble making friends.

5. The *bullied bully* is both a target and a bully. Bullied and abused by adults or older kids, she bullies others to get some relief from her own feelings of powerlessness and self-loathing. Least popular of all the bullies, she strikes out viciously at those who hurt her and at weaker or smaller targets.

6. The *bunch of bullies* is a group of friends who collectively do something they would never do individually to someone they want to exclude or scapegoat. Bullying, done by a group of "nice" kids who know that what they did was wrong and that it hurts their target, is still bullying.

7. The *gang of bullies* is a scary lot drawn together not as a

group of friends, but as a strategic alliance in pursuit of power, control, domination, subjugation, and turf. Initially joining to feel a part of a family of sorts, to be respected and to be protected, in their zeal they become so devoted to their group that they disregard their own lives, the carnage they inflict on their victims, and the overall consequences of their actions. Added to this zeal is a lack of empathy and remorse.

Although their ways and means of bullying may be different, bullies have these traits in common. They all:

1. like to dominate other people.
2. like to use other people to get what they want.
3. find it hard to see a situation from the other person's vantage point.
4. are concerned only with their own wants and pleasures and not the needs, rights, and feelings of others.
5. tend to hurt other kids when parents or other adults are not around.
6. view weaker siblings or peers as prey (bullying is also known as "predatory aggression"—a scary term, to be sure, but not as scary as the actual behaviour it defines).
7. use blame, criticism, and false allegations to project their own inadequacies onto their target.
8. refuse to accept responsibility for their actions.
9. lack foresight—that is, the ability to consider the short-term, long-term, and possible unintended consequences of their current behaviour.
10. crave attention.

Contempt Is the Key

You may have noticed that in this discussion of bullies, I haven't mentioned anger. Bullying is not about anger. It's not even about conflict. It's about contempt—a powerful feeling of dislike toward somebody considered to be worthless, inferior, or undeserving of respect. Contempt comes packaged with three *apparent* psychological advantages that allow kids to harm another human being without feeling empathy, compassion, or shame:

1. a sense of entitlement—the privilege and right to control, dominate, subjugate, and otherwise abuse another human being;
2. an intolerance toward differences—different equals inferior and thus not worthy of respect;
3. a liberty to exclude—to bar, isolate, and segregate a person deemed not worthy of respect or care.

In other words, bullying is arrogance in action. Kids who bully have an air of superiority that is often a mask to cover up deep hurt and a feeling of inadequacy. They rationalize that their supposed superiority entitles them to hurt someone they hold in contempt, when in reality it is an excuse to put someone down so they can feel "up".

Just as bullying can range from mild to moderate to severe, so contempt can range from disregard to scorn to hate. The biases at the foundation of this contempt are often deeply rooted attitudes found in our homes, our schools, and our society. Any bias or prejudice related to race, gender (including sexual orientation), religion, physical attributes, or mental abilities can and will be used by a bully to validate and justify contempt for an individual child or a group of children.

In his profoundly moving book, *Convicted in the Womb: One Man's Journey from Prisoner to Peacemaker*, Carl Upchurch, an elementary-school dropout, former gang member, ex-convict, and now author and respected community leader in the civil rights movement, wrote about "institutionalized racism" and its impact on him as a young child.

> The contempt for my people—every assumption, insult, and slur—was trimmed and tailored for my infant shoulders before I was born. . . . It took me more than thirty years to learn that, unlike being male or being black, being nigger wasn't coded into my DNA. . . . I grew up believing that I deserved society's contempt just because I was black. . . . I was governed by a careless, heartless ruthlessness fostered by a pervasive sense of inferiority.

By his own admission, Carl was a bullied bully. The careless, heartless ruthlessness was the hard shell he wrapped himself in to protect the quiet, gentle, sensitive child he was from the disregard, scorn, and hate he was subjected to regularly.

The Masquerade of Deception

Individual incidents of verbal, physical, or relational bullying can appear trivial or insignificant, nothing to be overly concerned about, part of the school culture. But it is the imbalance of power, the intent to harm, the threat of further aggression, and the creation of an atmosphere of terror that should raise red flags and signal a need for intervention. Sadly, even when the four markers of bullying are clearly in evidence, adults have been known to minimize or dismiss the bullying, underestimate its seriousness, blame the bullied child, and/or heap on additional insult to injury.

POWER PLAYS IN THE SCHOOL YARD:
CORRUPTING, COLLUDING, AND A CON JOB

Eight-year-old Meghan was suspended from school for pulling her trousers down in the playground in front of a group of boys while a group of girls watched. One child reported the incident to the supervizing teacher. When the teacher arrived on the scene, most of the boys and girls were laughing at Meghan. The teacher grabbed Meghan's arm and marched her into the principal's office, all the while telling her how ashamed she should be of her outrageous behaviour. The principal couldn't get Meghan to tell her why she would do such a thing. Meghan just sat in the chair in front of the principal's desk, shrugged her shoulders, and stared off into the distance.

When her father arrived, he found Meghan curled up in the office chair, sobbing. The principal suggested that the father get some help for his daughter, who was corrupting others in the playground by "exposing" herself. The father brought Meghan home and tried to comfort her and find out what had really happened. Having no luck, he called a family friend who was a social worker. The friend took Meghan to lunch and got the facts from this distraught second-grader.

Behind in reading since first grade, called "stupid" and "dumb", often excluded from her peers' play circles and parties, Meghan was desperate to belong to the popular group. The leader told her she could join the group if she would pull her trousers down in front of the boys; if she didn't, the bigger girl would make sure nobody else played with her. Corruption, yes, but the wrong player had been accused.

When confronted with the facts, Meridith (the bully) denied ever telling Meghan (the bullied) to do such a thing. Then she got the other girls (the bystanders) to go along with her by threatening to hurt them if they told anybody the truth. Finally, one girl, Julie, (a bystander turned witness), was so upset by the whole ordeal that she told her mum what had really happened and what was still going on at recess. In taking that risk, knowing that her mum would believe her, Julie started a chain of events at school that would make a world of difference for Meghan, Meridith, and their classmates—a difference that Meghan's suspension never could make. Meghan was fortunate to have a girl in her class who was willing to stand up, speak out, and support her.

HAZING: "IT'S PART OF THE GAME"

Brian was not as fortunate as Meghan. In 1993, Brian, a teenage football player, was dragged out of the locker-room shower and taped naked to the horizontal towel rack by five of his teammates. His hands, feet, chest, and genitals were bound with athletic tape. Then the five boys brought a girl Brian had once dated into the locker room to see him hanging from the towel rack. When the incident was reported to the administration, the team was banned from the high school regional playoffs. The season was over for the boys, but the bullying for Brian was not. Players, other students, parents, and community members felt the penalty was too severe; they argued that the humiliation Brian suffered was "part of the game". "It happens all the time." "It's been going on since we were sophomores . . . nobody told us not to do it." "It was just a joke." Brian was called abusive names, shunned, and shoved by classmates. He, not his five teammates, was blamed for the cancellation of the rest of the season. He was kicked off the football squad apparently for not apologizing to the team for "ratting on them".

Although Brian's parents supported him through the whole episode, peer backlash, community outrage, and the lack of administrative support compounded the humiliation and pain of the original incident.

Is hazing bullying? More often than not, it has the markers of bullying: imbalance of power (including the target of the hazing being outnumbered or lower on the social ladder than those doing the hazing); intent to harm (being forced to drink or exercise until passing out, being beaten or made to beat someone else); and threat of further aggression (being forced to eat disgusting things, to be tattooed, pierced, or shaved, or to steal or commit a crime "or else"). Not knowing what will happen next or when it will stop is a recipe for terror.

In an article about hazing in *USA Today*, Tamara Henry cited an April 2000 study by Alfred University, New York, concerning the "risk of initiations that include being humiliated or forced to engage in illegal or dangerous activities" when high-school kids join sports teams; music, art, and theatre groups; scholastic or intellectual clubs; and church groups. Of the 1,541 high-school students who responded to the random survey, 48 percent said they were subjected to hazing. The statistics are disturbing: 43 percent reported being subjected to humiliating activities, 23 percent were involved in substance abuse, and 29 percent told of performing potentially illegal acts.

"Our culture views hazing as 'fun and exciting'. America's obsession with 'fun' apparently gives us licence to justify almost any type of behaviour, no matter how abusive," said Robert Meyers, anthropology professor at Alfred.

"We anticipated that we would find some level of hazing," said Nadine Hoover, principal investigator. "What we found distressing was the prevalence."

We have to wonder why it is considered "fun and exciting" to demean another human being. We speak out of both sides of our mouth when we tell children not to bully one another in the playground, then encourage or condone hazing, calling it "character building" and "just part of the game".

It is important for all of us to feel that we belong. It can be such a powerful force for young people that they often will do unspeakably cruel things to themselves and other people in order to be accepted into a group. Rites of initiation can be powerful and meaningful. They do not have to be humiliating or demeaning. One problem of our modern culture is that we have not developed healthy, appropriately rigorous rites and rituals to mark the passage from childhood into adulthood. The Alfred University hazing study involved school- and church-sanctioned youth groups—groups that could be places to foster more healthy initiation rites.

CLIQUES AND THE SCHOOL SOCIAL LADDER

To gain acceptance and security during the preteen years and throughout their teens, kids not only join groups, they form groups called cliques, which have a commonality of interests, values, abilities, and tastes. This is good. There is also exclusivity and exclusion. This is not good. School cultures that nurture cliques and elevate some groups above others also nurture discrimination and bullying.

The comments made to the police by the student-body president of Columbine High School demonstrated how such a school culture can reinforce a sense of community by erecting strong walls to comfort and protect those on the inside. For those cast outside those exclusive walls, such a culture can mean systematic abuse, denial of equal protection, and an everyday life that is frightening and/or unbearable. Kids who don't fit into the honoured and revered cliques are often subjected to cruel and persistent bullying by members of these groups. The student-body president was quoted as saying that "all the 'sports type' kids referred to Dylan and Eric as the 'no sports'." He knew these kids got picked on all the time and that most of it was done by members of the football team.

Having been taunted, shunned, and physically bullied, "outsiders" often turn to other groups that will accept them. Tensions can rise between two cliques that are at the opposite ends of the social ladder. Administrations in such settings either turn a blind eye to the abuse heaped on the lower group by the upper echelon, reinforce it, or contribute to it by denying the problem. When asked about the apparent "jock culture" at the school, an administrator was quoted in the local newspaper as saying, "The only jock culture at Columbine are staph infections" (aka "jock itch").

After the videotapes shot by Dylan and Eric were made public well over a year after the shootings, there was still a sense of entitlement and superiority expressed by at least one member of the Columbine football team. In his mind, he had a right to taunt and torment anyone who was "different", anyone for whom he had contempt: "Columbine is a good, clean place except for those rejects. Most kids don't want them here. They were into witchcraft. They were into voodoo. Sure we teased them. But what do you expect with kids who come to school with weird hairdos and horns on their hats? It's not just jocks; the whole school's disgusted with them. They're a bunch of homos . . . If you want to get rid of someone, usually you tease 'em. So the whole school would call them homos. . . ."

In a column in *The Denver Post* shortly after the Columbine shootings, Chuck Green wrote, "Even as the shots were being fired, Columbine killers Eric Harris and Dylan Klebold were making one of their motives very, very clear: They resented the caste system at the high school, where popular athletes were provided star status. 'Jocks', as the athletes are commonly called, were at the top of the social order at Columbine, worshiped as the dukes of their campus fiefdom. In the first few days after the shootings, other students voiced similar concerns—that there was a class structure at Columbine, perpetuated by students and tolerated by administrators, that favoured major-sport athletes over common students."

The jock culture problem obviously extended beyond "jock itch". Green went on to expose a case involving one of the most popular student athletes. Courted by the likes of Stanford,

Harvard, and Colorado University, this student was also an accused stalker and prowler. He had been under a restraining order to stay away from his ex-girlfriend, also a student at Columbine. The student declined violence counselling and planned to fight the criminal charges.

Rather than focus on keeping the athlete—and alleged stalker—away from the girl, the administrators at Columbine proposed another solution: "The girl could leave school now—three weeks before graduation—with no penalty, to avoid contact with the football star. It would leave no mark on her record." No penalty and no mark on *her* record for being told to stay home? It is a strange though all too common way to treat the target of a bully.

Chuck Green's column did make a difference. After reading the column, administrators from the school district's central office asked for an inquiry and a detailed report. School board members demanded a full explanation of the facts in the case and reasserted the need for school administrators to pay more attention to intimidation and harassment of students and gender equity issues.

In a letter to the superintendent of schools, board member David DiGiacomo wrote, "This isn't the first time issues like this have come up, and we need to be more attentive to them. The problem isn't limited to Columbine. I'm convinced it is a systematic problem in most school districts."

Cindy Key, a parent of elementary-age children, voiced the concern of many parents in the district: "Our main issue is that respect and tolerance need to be taught in our schools, and it should begin in grade school. We are concerned about bullying and teasing, and taunting. We can spend all the money in the world on security *around* the school, but it won't do much good if students don't feel safe *inside* the school."

RACIST BULLYING: A DOUBLE WHAMMY

In *The Anti-Bullying Handbook*, New Zealand professor Keith Sullivan, internationally recognized for his work in bullying prevention programmes, described what happens when racist attitudes collide with bullying.

Rangi is working by himself in the classroom. The door opens. "What are you doing, Maori boy?" taunts David. "Did ya fall in the shit, black boy?" He struts closer. "Are you reading something? I didn't know you could read." "Hey, nigger," the other boys say as they start to filter in and see Rangi on his own. Instead of ignoring these taunts and provocations (as he has done four or five times over the last month), Rangi loses his temper. He turns on David. The two boys fight and Rangi is clearly the better fighter and is winning. David's friend Jim steps in, grabs Rangi around the neck, and pulls him away from David, throwing him on the ground. He helps David up. The duty [supervizing] teacher arrives, and David and Rangi are taken to the deputy principal's office. David has been crying and says that he was just having fun and that Rangi went "psycho" and really hurt him. When questioned, Rangi is surly and insolent and is suspended from school for a week for fighting and being rude to the deputy principal. David's friends back him up and say that Rangi went "psycho" for no apparent reason. David is given a warning about fighting but is largely seen as the innocent party.

Rangi is identified by those in authority as the aggressor. He is not listened to. Instead, the boy with more credibility in the school is believed.

Dr Sullivan went on to point out that although there is a strong element of racism in the bullying event, the school authorities had previously stated that racism did not exist at their school. They believe the bully and punish the bullied boy for fighting back. The boys will probably not bully Rangi again; rather, they will find someone they can bully more easily. Yet their racist attitudes have not been challenged. Rangi will probably nurse a grudge against the boys, rage against the injustice, and turn against the school because of its inability to address the problem justly.

Maori children are in the minority in this South Island school, as well as being oppressed First Nations people of New Zealand. Replace Maori with Dene, Inuit, Cherokee, Blackfoot, Navajo, Hopi, Lakota, Sioux, or any other racial or ethnic minority and you see a similar picture of what is happening in many schools across the United States, Canada and the UK.

Racist bullying doesn't just happen. Kids have to be taught to be racist before they can engage in racist bullying. Racist bullying takes place in a climate where children are taught to discriminate against a group of people, where differences are seen as bad, and where the common bonds of humanity are not celebrated.

Children systematically learn the language of racial slurs and the rules of bigoted behaviour through thought (stereotype), feeling (prejudice), and action (discrimination). First, children are taught to *stereotype*—that is, to generalize about an entire group of people without regard to individual differences: [insert a group] are hot-tempered, ugly, lazy, stupid, no good, crazy . . .

Second, children are taught to *prejudge* a person based on this stereotype. Prejudice is a feeling: We don't like [————].

Combine racist thought and feeling and you get children willing to *discriminate* against individuals in that group: You can't play with us. You can't come to our party. We don't want you on our team. Get out of here, you creep!

This is bullying and needs to be addressed as such. It is only a short walk from racist discrimination to scapegoating a particular child—selecting someone to suffer in place of others or attaching blame or wrongdoing to a specific child when it is not clear who is at fault. Rangi was accused of starting the fight because "his kind" have hot tempers.

Getting Caught

The incident with David and Rangi demonstrates not only what often happens when a bullied child strikes back, but also what a bully tends to do when called to account:

1. Deny that he did anything wrong.
2. Trivialize the event: "I was just having some fun with him."
3. Counterattack: "He just went 'psycho' on us."
4. Claim victim status by crying and accusing the other kid of starting the episode. This usually provokes the bullied child (who, in Rangi's case, had taken abuse for over a month before finally striking back. Rangi was surly and insolent when questioned).

5. Get off the hook by casting the bullied kid as the bully. David is seen as the innocent party.
6. Count on the support of the bystanders to deny anything the bullied kid says in defence of his actions. David's friends back him up, saying that Rangi went "psycho" for no apparent reason.

The bully learned his lines well, mastered the ability to act the part of the wronged party, got others to collude with him, and played on both the emotions and biases of the adults. The cycle of violence continues.

When it comes to racism, school policy, procedures, and prevention programmes have to work hand in hand. Step one is to acknowledge that racist attitudes exist in our schools. Then we can be open to the possibility that racist bullying is happening inside those walls as well. (Chapter Nine will look at school policies, procedures, and prevention programmes that can work against bullying in general and racist and sexist bullying in particular.)

A Comedy Is Not a Prelude to a Tragedy— Teasing Is Not Taunting

In many of the stories in the introduction, kids were bullied with words, taunted about their race, religion, gender, physical attributes, or mental abilities. (These categories are known as the "big five" when it comes to attacking someone effectively.) It's difficult to teach children that teasing is a normal part of healthy human relationships and at the same time tell them that if they tease someone else, they could be called to account for bullying. It's even more difficult to teach children to stop teasing when it becomes harmful, hurtful, and no longer fun. It is more helpful to give kids two different words to describe two different activities. When kids understand that one is a part of having fun with friends and the other is outright bullying, we can reduce the excuses "I was just teasing" and "Can't you take a joke?". By learning the unique characteristics of teasing and taunting, and giving each its own name, kids will be able to label what they are doing and understand more clearly why one is acceptable and the other is not.

Teasing is a fun thing you do with friends—with people you care about. Taunting is a choice to bully someone for whom you have contempt. Identifying taunting as bullying communicates the gravity and meanness of it to the bully and any bystanders who might be inclined to join in the cruel game, and it lends credibility to the pain the bullied child experiences.

Teasing

1. Allows the teaser and person teased to swap roles with ease.
2. Isn't intended to hurt the other person.
3. Maintains the basic dignity of everyone involved.
4. Pokes fun in a lighthearted, clever, and benign way.
5. Is meant to get both parties to laugh.
6. Is only a small part of the activities shared by kids who have something in common.
7. Is innocent in motive.
8. Is discontinued when person teased becomes upset or objects to the teasing.

When kids tease one another, there is a playfulness that is not present in taunting. Both give it and take it equally. If a child inadvertently says something that is hurtful to her friend, perhaps intending to wrap in humour something that is difficult to say outright, she picks up on her mistake by reading her friend's hurt and makes amends. The two are learning important lessons in relationship building and effective communication. They can practise with each other and safely learn limits and boundaries of teasing, as well as the power of words. They share strong feelings of affection, compassion, and empathy. If they laugh at each other's foibles and mistakes, they are just as quick to be there to help the other clean up the mess. Good-natured ribbing reflects the closeness of two friends' relationship. Off limits are attacks about race, religion, gender, physical attributes, or mental ability. Any attack is not teasing; it is taunting.

Taunting

1. Is based on an imbalance of power and is one-sided: the bully taunts, the bullied kid is taunted.
2. Is intended to harm.
3. Involves humiliating, cruel, demeaning, or bigoted comments thinly disguised as jokes.
4. Includes laughter directed *at* the target, not *with* the target.
5. Is meant to diminish the sense of self-worth of the target.
6. Induces fear of further taunting or can be a prelude to physical bullying.
7. Is sinister in motive.
8. Continues especially when targeted kid becomes distressed or objects to the taunt.

When a bully taunts her target, there is no playfulness in the attack, no matter how much the bully may protest, "I was just teasing". The bullied kid was probably targeted because the bully knew he or she would not strike back. There is no good-natured give-and-take. The taunt is intended to isolate the target. It is intended to hurt, and the words used are demeaning and cruel. The bully may laugh, and so might the bystanders. The target is embarrassed, humiliated, or shamed, living in fear of what will come next. There is no empathy or compassion; rather, there is glee, excitement, or amusement over the success of the attack. The motive of the bully is not to make a new friend, engage in friendly banter, or lighten a difficult situation; it is purely to belittle and demean another child.

A Little About Sex, a Lot About Contempt— Sexual Bullying

Just as racist attitudes can collide with bullying, so, too, can sexist attitudes. And all three forms of bullying—physical, verbal, and relational—can be wrapped in sexual overtones. Because our sexuality is an integral part of who we are, sexual bullying cuts at the core of our being and can have devastating consequences. Peer-to-peer sexual bullying is one of the most widespread forms of violence in our schools today. According to the 1993 "Hostile Hallways" study conducted by the American Association of University Women Educational Foundation, questionnaire responses of 1,632 students from grades eight to eleven offered some startling information:

- 85 percent of girls and 76 percent of boys reported having

experienced sexual harassment.
- 65 percent of girls reported being touched, grabbed, or pinched in a sexual way.
- 13 percent of girls and 9 percent of boys reported being forced to do something sexual other than kissing.
- 25 percent of girls stayed home from school or cut classes to avoid sexual harassment.
- 86 percent of girls targeted reported being sexually harassed by their peers.
- 25 percent of girls targeted reported being sexually harassed by school staff.

One third of the kids surveyed reported experiencing sexual bullying in sixth grade or earlier. Boys and girls reported experiencing sexual harassment in the hallway (73 percent), in the classroom (65 percent), in the school grounds (48 percent), and in the cafeteria (34 percent). The study pointed to serious educational consequences as well as significant threats to the physical and emotional well-being of targeted kids. Girls who mature early and boys who mature late are at a high risk for being targeted for sexual bullying. Kids of different sexual orientation from the majority are likely to be bullied. In the article "Young, Gay, and Bullied" (*Young People Now*), researcher I. Rivers wrote about his 1996 study, in which he interviewed 140 gay and lesbian young people. He found that 80 percent of those responding had experienced taunting about their sexual orientation, and over half had been physically assaulted or ridiculed by peers or teachers.

VERBAL SEXUAL BULLYING

Verbal bullying is the most common form of bullying, so it would make sense that the most common form of sexual bullying would be verbal. It can stand alone but is often the entrée to physical sexual bullying or relational sexual bullying and is too often the first step toward more vicious and degrading sexual violence. The nature of this type of bullying is different for boys and girls. The words used to bully boys tend to be derogatory terms defining them as "less than a boy"—that is, a girl (sissy, wuss, pussy, bitch, "you run like a girl")—or homophobic terms (gay, fag, queer, homo, "light in his loafers"). The words used to bully girls tend to objectify their bodies, demean their sexuality, or infantilize them (fat, dog, "eight", cunt, hole, pussy, lez, slut, whore, hooker, babe, baby, chick, kitten). Verbal bullying can also include threats to sexually violate the target, verbal assessments of the target's body, sexist or sexual jokes, or derogatory comments about sexual performance or lack of sexual activity.

Just as bullies who taunt their peers will argue that they intended no harm—were just teasing—so too do bullies who add sexist or sexual overtones to their bullying plead that they were only flirting. If kids are taught the difference between teasing and taunting, they are more readily able to distinguish between flirting and sexual bullying.

Flirting

1. Allows and invites both persons to swap roles with ease.
2. Isn't intended to hurt the other person—is an expression of desire.
3. Maintains the basic dignity of both persons.

4. Is meant to be flattering and complimentary.
5. Is an invitation to have fun together and enjoy each other's company.
6. Invites sexual attention.
7. Is intended to make the other person feel wanted, attractive, and in control.
8. Is discontinued when the person who is being flirted with becomes upset, objects to the flirting, or is not interested.

Flirting has playfulness about it that sexual bullying does not. It is never intended to harm and is an invitation for two people to get to know each other better. As with any other invitation, it can be accepted or rejected—and the person who initiated the flirting honours either response.

Sexual Bullying

1. Is based on an imbalance of power and is one-sided: the bully sexually taunts, the bullied kid is demeaned and degraded.
2. Is intended to harm and exploit.
3. Is invasive and intended to assert the status of the bully.
4. Is intended to be degrading or demeaning.
5. Is intended to express control and domination.
6. Is intended to violate the boundaries of the target.
7. Is intended to make the other person feel rejected, ugly, degraded, powerless, or uncomfortable.
8. Continues especially when targeted kid becomes distressed or objects to the sexual comment.

In sexual bullying there is no invitation—just an attack. The target is embarrassed, humiliated, and shamed and tends to feel powerless. It is not the intention of the bully to engage in healthy sexual flirtation with another person—the attack is meant to hurt. If the target protests, he or she is often labelled a "bitch" who is uptight and can't take a joke.

PHYSICAL SEXUAL BULLYING

Physical sexual bullying can include, but is certainly not limited to, touching or grabbing in a sexual way, pinching, bra snapping, pulling down trousers or pulling up skirts, brushing against a target in a sexual way, or "sexual assault". It is important to note that criminal activity can have sexual bullying as one of its components. In October 2001, a sixth-grade girl in Denver, Colorado, was sexually bullied and assaulted in a middle-school computer lab where twenty-four students were working in groups. A twelve-year-old boy held a knife to the girl's leg and offered three friends $5 to be the first to fondle or grope their classmate. The three boys touched the girl all over her body, the girl's mother said in the complaint filed with the school district. According to the news report, "The teacher did not see what happened and thought the four boys and the girl were friends."

RELATIONAL SEXUAL BULLYING

Add sexual overtones to all the ways kids use relational bullying to systematically diminish a bullied child's sense of self-worth—sexual rumours or sexual epithets on toilet walls or lockers, shunning a target because of his or her sexual orientation, "scanning" a target's body, staring at breasts, leering, or making obscene gestures—and what you have is a hard-to-detect, easy-to-execute method of cutting to the core of the bullied kid. Add to all of these the displaying or circulating of sexually explicit material intended to shame or humiliate or degrade, the wearing of clothes or badges that have sexually offensive sayings or pictures, or the existence of sexually explicit graffiti, and you have the ingredients for creating what the Canadian Human Rights Commission (1991) and the United States Civil Rights Act of 1964 identified as a hostile environment that interferes with a student's ability to learn. [2]

In 1992, a Minnesota school principal ignored a girl's request to remove from a boys' toilet sexually explicit and lewd graffiti about her. When the graffiti was not removed after two years of complaining, the girl filed a suit against the school district. The district reportedly settled the case for $15,000. Two years and $15,000 later appears to be a social commentary on a school climate that tolerates—if not invites—the dehumanization and degradation of a portion of its population who are required to be there every day.

A New York middle-school teacher and author of *Sexual Respect Curriculum*, Peter Milner sums up the difference between healthy expressions of sexuality and sexual bullying: "Can you espouse the values of fairness and respect, and at the same time discriminate and injure? Sexist and sexually harassing behaviours are dissatisfying and therefore undesirable actions that hurt people and are unworthy of people of intelligence and integrity."

---

[2] In Europe, after World War II, the European Convention on Human Rights set out important basic human rights. This was incorporated into British domestic law in the Human Rights Act of 1998, which came into force on 2 October 2000. Article 3 confers the right (of all individuals , including children) to be free from torture, inhuman or degrading treatment or punishment.

What Bullying Is Not

As you can see, taunting is not merely an act of aggression; it has the markers of bullying. Sexual bullying is not even related to flirting, and no matter what form it takes, it is an act of aggression. Not all acts of aggression are bullying—some are less serious than bullying and some more serious. Although bullying is the focus of this book, it is helpful to know what bullying is not. The distinctions are not always so obvious at first glance.

Bullying does not include normal childhood behaviours such as sibling rivalry or one-on-one fighting of siblings or peers with competing claims. Nor does it include acts of impulsive aggression—in other words, aggression that is a spontaneous, indiscriminate striking out, with no intended target. Such aggression is often related to a physical or mental handicap, such as autism or Asperger's syndrome (high functioning autism), and must not be dismissed or excused, but it is not bullying. Spontaneous, deliberate, indiscriminate striking out also may be a response by a bullied kid to an attack by a bully, but it is not bullying (more on this in the next chapter).

At the other end of the spectrum, bullying does not include criminal activities that may have begun as a conflict and escalated. These may include serious physical assault, a serious threat of physical assault, assault with a weapon, and vandalism. These require legal intervention as well as disciplinary procedures and therapeutic intervention, but they are not bullying. However, it is important to note that some violent activities bear the markers of bullying as well as of criminality. These are commonly called hate crimes: criminal acts against a person, group of people, or property in which the bully chooses the target because of the target's real or perceived race, religion, sexual orientation, national origin, disability, gender, or ethnicity. Not only do these require legal intervention, they require disciplinary procedures and therapeutic intervention that address the elements of contempt and arrogance that are packaged with the violence.

It does not matter if it is mild, moderate, or severe: bullying is *not normal*. It is *antisocial* and needs to be addressed as such. This is why current zero-tolerance policies (those that attempt to respond to a one-on-one fight, bullying, and assault with one solution—expulsion) are really zero-thinking policies. Such policies are about efficiency and finding fault, not about effective solutions for breaking the cycle of violence. What needs to be found is a *social solution to this antisocial activity*.

In order to practise being bullies, kids need to find other kids to bully. Whom they find may surprise you. The next chapter looks at "the bullied"—who they are, how they respond, and the potential impact of bullying on their lives.

> *Hatred deforms the hater more than the hated. As if any enemy could be more hurtful than the hatred with which he has incensed against him; or could wound more deeply him whom he persecutes, than he wounds his own soul by his enmity.*

> —St Augustine (fifth-century bishop)

CHAPTER THREE

The Bullied

Don't laugh at me, don't call me names,
Don't take your pleasure from my pain.
I'm a little boy with glasses
The one they call a geek,
A little girl who never smiles
'Cause I have braces on my teeth
And I know how it feels to cry myself to sleep
I'm that kid on every playground
Who's always chosen last
A single teenage mother
Tryin' to overcome my past
You don't have to be my friend
But is it too much to ask: Don't laugh at me
Don't call me names
Don't get your pleasure from my pain . . .
Don't laugh at me I'm fat, I'm thin, I'm short, I'm tall
I'm deaf, I'm blind, hey aren't we all.

—Steve Seskin and Allen Shamblin,
"Don't Laugh at Me"

Just like bullies, kids who are bullied come in all sizes and shapes. Some are big, some are small; some bright and some not so bright; some attractive and some not so attractive; some popular and some disliked by almost everybody. The one thing that all kids who are bullied have in common is that they were targeted by a bully (or by a bunch of bullies). Each one was singled out to be the object of scorn and thus the recipient of verbal, physical, or relational aggression, merely because he or she was different in some way. Bullies need targets on whom they can heap their aggression, and the differences identified as the justifications for the attacks are spurious at best, contemptuous excuses at worst.

The myths that abound in our society about targets—weak and pathetic, frail, insecure, loner, in a "dance" with a bully, asking to be bullied, had it coming, deserving of what they got, "losers deserve to lose"—all feed into the rationalizations kids (and many adults) make for not putting the onus for the bullying on the bully, for joining in, for turning away from the targets, or worse, for blaming the targets for what happened to them. No one deserves to be bullied.

Kids who have behaviours that annoy or amuse their peers still have a right to be treated with dignity and respect, just like anyone else. Granted, they may need to change their behaviours or, as in the case with children who have Asperger's syndrome (high functioning autism), may need to memorize the clues that other kids read instinctively so as to not so readily be made the fool by peers who think it's okay to play tricks on them. We need to ask why kids would feel they have a right to disregard, scorn, or hate another kid simply because that child was different in some way from themselves. Why would kids take their pleasure from another kid's pain?

In *Protecting the Gift: Keeping Children and Teenagers Safe (And Parents Sane)* by Gavin de Becker, Dr Mary Arneson details her experiences as a child with mild autism:

> It is a world of people who act friendly and then turn out to be enemies. School is a place where people do mean things all the time, for no reason. The things that matter most, or are the source of most comfort, are objects of ridicule. For example, the autistic child dresses to please herself. In my case, the problem was that girls simply did not wear roomy shoes, and I simply did not wear shoes that hurt . . . so I chose boys' tennis shoes. . . . Other kids could have ignored this, but they didn't. What I remember, instead, is a girl phoning me and saying that she really admired my shoes I wore and asking where she could get some. Unsuspecting, I told her, not realizing that my believing anyone could admire those shoes was the funniest thing she and the other girls listening on the line could imagine.

Kids with autism often walk with an unusual gait, have narrow, focused interests, and don't read social cues well. They are easy targets for kids to mimic their gait, mock their interests, and persuade them to act in ways that get them in trouble— entertainment for the bullies.

When a bully feels a need to put someone down in order to feel superior herself (or to confirm her already superior status), it doesn't take much to find an excuse to target someone. Targets can be just about anybody:

1. The kid who is new on the block.
2. The kid who is the youngest in the school—and thus usually smaller, sometimes scared, maybe insecure. Bullying escalates when a new class enters middle school or high school.
3. The kid who has been traumatized—who is already hurt by a prior trauma, is extremely sensitive, avoids peers to avoid further pain, and finds it hard to ask for help.
4. The kid who is submissive—who is anxious, lacking in self-confidence, and easily led and who does things to please or placate others.
5. The kid who has behaviours others find annoying.
6. The kid who is unwilling to fight—who prefers to resolve conflicts without aggression.
7. The kid who is shy, reserved, quiet or unassuming, timid, sensitive.
8. The kid who is poor or rich.
9. The kid whose race or ethnicity is viewed by the bully as inferior, deserving of contempt.
10. The kid whose gender/sexual orientation is viewed by the bully as inferior, deserving of contempt.
11. The kid whose religion is viewed by the bully as inferior, deserving of contempt.
12. The kid who is bright, talented, or gifted—targeted because she "stands out"—in other words, is different.
13. The kid who is independent and unconcerned about social status, doesn't conform to the norm.
14. The kid who expresses emotions readily.
15. The kid who is fat or thin, short or tall.
16. The kid who wears braces or glasses.

17. The kid who has acne or any other skin condition.
18. The kid who has superficial physical attributes that are different from those of the majority.
19. The kid with physical and/or mental disabilities—such children are two to three times more likely to be bullied than other kids because they have an obvious disability and thus a ready excuse for the bully; they are not as well integrated into classes and thus have fewer friends to come to their aid; and they lack verbal and/or physical skills to adequately defend themselves against the aggression. A child with attention deficit hyperactivity disorder may act before he thinks, not reflecting on the possible consequences of his behaviour and, purposely or inadvertently, annoying a bully.
20. The kid who is in the wrong place at the wrong time— attacked because the bully wanted to aggress on someone right there, right now.

Alexandra Shea tells of the power bullies can have over kids who are different from the "norm". Describing herself as an "admittedly shy, reclusive, and somewhat peculiar only child", she wrote of her fears about going to summer camp. Number four on her list:

Them—the junior capos who run the social underground in these rustic gulags. *They* are the bully-princesses who have always abounded in Grade 6 female society. Their hair is perfect, their clothes ditto, and *They* decide who is in and who is condemned to the outer darkness, the subject of ridicule, whispers, and ostracism. I knew instinctively on which side of the great divide I would fall.

... I had a gut instinct that books were not highly
regarded as a suitable pastime and that bookish kids came
just after rabies-riddled raccoons in the pecking order. Oh
yes ... I was an odd child indeed.

("What I Didn't Do at Summer Camp",
Globe and Mail, May 28, 2001)

Almost all of us have been on the receiving end of some sort of
bullying, even if we ourselves were bullies—in fact, especially if
we were bullies. As you will see in Chapter Five, bullies learn to
be bullies in large part by the way they were treated by bigger or
more powerful people in their lives. In her book *For Your Own
Good*, internationally renowned psychiatrist Dr Alice Miller
writes: "It is very difficult for people to believe the simple fact
that every persecutor was once a victim. Yet it should be very
obvious that someone who is allowed to feel free and strong from
childhood does not have the need to humiliate another person."

To feel free and strong applies not just to the bully. It is a
necessary ingredient for any kid to thrive. As shown in "Scenes
from a Tragedy" on page 6, kids who bully, who are targets, and
who are bystanders are all bound up in the cycle of violence and
weakened by the experience. The myths about who is the target
of bullying often are based on what a bullied kid looks and acts
like *after* having been bullied repeatedly.

Once she has been targeted by the bully, how a child responds
will influence whether or not she moves from target to victim.
Alexandra Shea was definitely affected by the "bully-princesses";
they were one of the four reasons she wanted to stay away from
camp. Yet she did not succumb to their ridicule, whispers, and
ostracism. She writes in her article, "With time and tender mercy,

I got better on my own. I now live a life replete with friends and abounding with joys. I am no longer shy." She also suggests that the bully-princesses don't always change when they grow up: "They are still with us, under a veneer of social civility, a thin one."

If a kid succumbs to the attack—gives the bully what is demanded by showing distress, fear, or apathy; or fails to respond assertively (or aggressively)—he changes both emotionally and physically. He becomes someone he was not before the attack; and all future attacks will be against this ever-weakening target. The guilt, shame, and sense of failure felt by a target unable to cope with the brutalization contribute to the destruction of his sense of well-being. As he becomes more isolated from his peers, has trouble concentrating on schoolwork, and develops survival strategies instead of social skills, his life changes radically. How bystanders respond to both the bully and the target has a tremendous influence on how emboldened the bully becomes and/or how weak the target gets.

Evan Ramsey, a target who became a victim, will be spending the rest of his life in prison. Trapped in the rigid social system of Bethal Regional High School in a remote town in Alaska, shy, small-framed Evan Ramsey was the target of abuse for years. Speaking to writer Ron Arias for the article "Disarming the Rage" (*People* magazine, June 4, 2001), he described the bullying: "Everybody had given me a nickname: Screech, the nerdy character on [television programme] *Saved by the Bell*. . . . I got stuff thrown at me, I got spit on, I got beat up. Sometimes I fought back, but I wasn't that good at fighting." At first he reported the incidents to his teachers. "After a while [the principal] told me to just start ignoring everybody. But then you can't take it any more."

On February 19, 1997, Evan walked into the high school with a twelve-gauge shotgun and killed schoolmate Josh Palacios and the principal, Ron Edwards. Evan was tried as an adult and sentenced to 210 years in prison. From his cell in the correctional centre in Seward, Alaska, he admits, "I felt a sense of power with a gun. It was the only way to get rid of the anger." Eligible for parole when he is eighty-six years old, Evan spoke a truth kids who have been bullied relentlessly know in their hearts and try to get adults to understand: "I would have had a different life if I hadn't been treated like that."

Another teenager was sentenced to eight and a half years for smuggling a duffel bag full of guns and bombs into Southside High School in Elmira, New York, on February 14, 2001. After years of being a target for bullies, Jeremy Getman intended to go on a killing spree but realized he couldn't kill innocent people and surrendered peacefully to the police. He said he knew what he did was wrong and that he deserved to be punished. "I truly believed everyone hated me, I felt confused, alone, and desperate. . . . I know in my heart I am not a killer."

In an interview for ABC News, Rachel, a teenager from Littleton, Colorado, said she could relate to the loneliness, abuse, and resentment felt by kids who plotted killings at their schools in retaliation for the cruel form of entertainment bullies enjoyed at their expense. Classmates tormented Rachel for five and a half years. "They actually had a contest. They'd high-five each other if they came up with the best name to describe how ugly I was. They'd kick me in the back of my knees and give me small bruises or they tripped me." A quiet girl, she became more withdrawn after each episode, locking herself in her room after school and crying. It was only after she transferred to another school that she could escape her tormentors. "I finally felt human again."

Rachel was able to move to a new school. Elizabeth Bush wasn't as fortunate. She will be spending the next few years as a ward of the court and is getting her schooling in a psychiatric facility. On March 7, 2001, in Williamsport, Pennsylvania, she brought her father's gun to school and shot another girl, wounding her in the shoulder. The shooting victim was Elizabeth's former friend, who had joined with the other girls who had taunted her repeatedly with such names as " idiot, stupid, fat, ugly". Making a daily practice of shunning and excluding her from their social circles, the bunch of bullies felt no remorse for what they had done. In fact, some failed to see how "just teasing her" could get her that upset. They didn't get it. Elizabeth, on the other hand, has expressed remorse and has taken full responsibility for her actions.

Shame, Secrets, and Sorrow

How could these situations reach such a point without any intervention, without an adult noticing? Why didn't these kids just tell somebody? In each of these stories, adults did know; kids did ask for help. Few got any relief. Parents are often the last to know. At the arraignment for Elizabeth Bush, her father told reporters, "We had no way of knowing how much she was taunted."

If your child is a target of a bully, don't count on him telling you about it outright: "Hey, guess what happened to me today!" It's not going to happen. Kids have many reasons for not telling adults about a bullying situation:

1. They are ashamed of being bullied. The bully intends to

make the target feel unworthy of respect, unpopular, isolated, and shamed. Boys are less likely than girls to tell an adult. Boys are culturally inculcated with the idea that they are supposed to "take it", "be strong", and "go it alone", in concert with "Don't cry" and "Don't go running to Mummy", two of society's traditional admonitions. Girls and boys are both unlikely to report sexual bullying and instead "put up with it", seeing it as an ugly part of the social and school culture that isn't going to change any time soon. Younger children are more likely to tell than older kids. Younger kids still think they can ask an adult to help and expect that adults will help. Older kids know that's not necessarily true and often have experience that would validate their thinking.

2. They are afraid of retaliation if they tell an adult. Bullies fuel this fear with threats. The fear and the implied or actual threats of retaliation combine to foster the "code of silence" that enables bullies to get away with their brutalizing activities.

3. They don't think anyone *can* help them. Feeling more and more isolated by the bullying, they believe that they are in this alone. The bully is too powerful, too sneaky, and too smart to be stopped.

4. They don't think anyone *will* help them. They are told to try to get along with the bully, to just stay out of his or her way, to fight back, and not to be a "wimp".

5. They have bought into the lie that bullying is a necessary part of growing up. It might hurt like hell, but the hell is part of the landscape of childhood.

6. They may believe that adults are part of the lie, since it is

not only kids who are bullying them. Some of the adults in their life may bully them, too. These adult bullies might have even given other kids "permission" to torment them, or at least sanctioned such behaviour.

7. They have learned that "ratting" on a peer is bad, not cool, "juvenile"—even if that peer is bullying them. "Sucking it up" (taking it) and just letting it go is supposed to be a more "mature" response to getting verbally abused, physically abused, or shunned.

Kids might not tell an adult outright that they are being bullied for any or all of the reasons listed above, but they usually give us clues. We just need to be tuned in to them. If your gut says it's happening, it probably is.

Kids speak in five ways: with body, face, eyes, tone of voice, and words. Sometimes their words are an excuse or cover for what they are really trying to say. Don't dismiss changes in your child's behaviour as merely a phase, something that will pass. Be alert to the frequency, duration, and intensity of any changes. Bullying can have long-term physical and psychological consequences. When you see warning signs, listen beyond the words, look beyond the actions, and try to put yourself in your child's shoes.

Warning Signs

1. Shows an abrupt lack of interest in school or a refusal to go to school. (According to a National Association of School Psychologists report, 160,000 children in the United States miss school every day for fear of being bullied. Why voluntarily get in the path of the school bullies?)

2. Takes an unusual route to school. (Going north and three blocks east to get to a school that is south of your home makes a lot of sense if going directly south will put you in the path of a bunch of bullies who have promised to beat you up, take your jacket, or relieve you of your lunch money.)

3. Suffers a drop in grades. (It's hard to concentrate on schoolwork when you are trying to figure out how to avoid the bullies, shaking in fear of what will happen next, and still recovering from the last attack. Later in the bullying cycle, your time and energy is used up plotting schemes to get revenge instead of doing a maths assignment.)

4. Withdraws from family and school activities, wanting to be left alone. (When you feel isolated, shamed, scared, and humiliated, you just want to curl up in a ball and not talk to anyone—or lock yourself in your room and cry.)

5. Is hungry after school, saying he lost his lunch money or wasn't hungry at school. (The bully takes great pleasure in extorting lunch money. The lunchroom ranks third behind the playground and hallways in the order of places where bullies attack their targets, so it's a good place to avoid, even if you do have your lunch money.)

6. Is taking parents' money and making lame excuses for where it went. (Once again the bully separates you from your money. The threats of retaliation can convince you that stealing from your mum's purse or your dad's wallet poses a lesser risk to body and mind than not showing up with the money for the bully.)

7. Makes a beeline to the toilet when she gets home. (Since

toilets are number four on the list of places bullies like to attack, you figure it's best to "hold on", even at risk of a bladder infection. A bladder infection can't possibly hurt as much as having your head dunked in a swirling toilet or seeing your reputation attacked via insulting graffiti on the mirrors over the sinks.)

8. Is sad, sullen, angry, or scared after receiving a phone call or an e-mail. (You don't know how to tell your mum or dad that the girls on the other end of the phone line called you ugly names and then all laughed before hanging up. You are ashamed to talk about the obscene lies the boy in your English class wrote about you and sent to everyone on his e-mail list. You are paralysed with fear after opening your e-mail. The bully assures you there is no escaping his taunts. What could your parents possibly do that would help and not make it worse?)

9. Does something out of character. (You would rather get caught skipping school than caught in the school yard by the bunch of bullies who circle around you every day and "pretend" to be playing. You would be willing to pull your trousers down at recess if those girls promise to quit taunting you and will let you into their social circle.)

10. Uses derogatory or demeaning language when talking about peers. (If you're being called ugly names, poked, shoved, shunned, and laughed at, you won't have any terms of endearment for the kids who started the bullying or for those who joined in or looked the other way. Who's left to talk about?)

11. Stops talking about peers and everyday activities. (If you're being bullied, you have no everyday activities that are not

coloured with pain, frustration, fear, and terror. What's left to talk about?)

12. Has dishevelled, torn, or missing clothing. (You don't like to resolve conflict by slugging it out, and it wasn't a one-on-one fight between equals with competing claims. But saying you got in a fight sounds better than saying you got beaten up, called ugly names, and threatened with further beatings if you told. Besides, the last time you told your dad about the bullying, he told you to fight back. Or you surrendered your favourite jacket rather than risk an attack, but saying that you "accidentally" left it in the locker room will go over better at home than admitting how you really lost it.)

13. Has physical injuries not consistent with explanation. (Saying that you walked into a locker sure sounds better than admitting you were shoved into one. Saying you sprained your ankle running to class beats revealing that those girls tripped you in the bus aisle, then laughed as you limped back to your seat. "I don't know how I got that black eye; I must have fallen out of bed," rings less painfully than recalling how you were held down and kicked in the face on the way to school.)

14. Has stomachaches, headaches, panic attacks, is unable to sleep, sleeps too much, is exhausted. (Bullies can be real pains on the brain and on the body. The body responds to the stress of being targeted by turning on its chemical defence system so you can fight or flee. But with daily attacks, this system can never shut down. Adrenalin keeps getting released. The body stays on hyperalert, churning up the stomach, twitching the limbs, and numbing the

brain. Constantly resisting and fearing the bully taxes the mental and physical defences. Eventually the system breaks down and the mind and body collapse into a state of exhaustion.)

Bullycide and Mayhem

Many kids—humiliated, embarrassed, battered, and shamed—wear a mask of normality every day, but underneath the fake smiles and nervous laughter is crushing hurt. If the pain is not relieved, the child may go into a tailspin, and the signs you will begin to see are far more alarming than those listed above. Tremendous shame brought on by rejection and humiliation can drive kids to implode or explode. James Garbarino, professor of human development at Cornell University and author of *Lost Boys: Why Our Sons Turn Violent and How We Can Save Them*, writes of the devastating effects of attacks on the core of a person's existence: "Shame imposes this fear that one will cease to exist, the prospect of psychic annihilation. Nothing seems to threaten the human spirit more than rejection, brutalization, and lack of love. Nothing . . . can equal insults to the soul." He goes on to explain that kids who are shamed are vulnerable to committing acts of violence and aggression, because such acts are a way of saying that they are not ciphers, that they do exist. In a tormented child's mind, the threat of psychic annihilation combined with a need to somehow respond to the injustice perpetrated by the actions of the bully and the inactions of peer and adult bystanders leaves him one choice—to strike out. Violence doesn't just happen. It is not unpredictable, nor does it come out of nowhere. It is the tragic ending of what is often a long, dramatic story, with small hints, red flags, and cries for help along the way.

In *Bullycide: Death at Playtime—An Exposé of Child Suicide Caused by Bullying*, Neil Marr and Tim Field coin the term *bullycide* to more accurately describe when bullied children choose to kill themselves rather than face one more day of being bullied. It was estimated in 2002 that at least sixteen children every year in the United Kingdom choose death over being battered by their peers. In 1999, roughly one out of every thirteen US high-school students reported making a suicide attempt in the previous twelve months—a rate that has tripled over the last twenty years. In the year 2000, more than two thousand kids succeeded. There are no statistics for how many of those two thousand were actually bullycides.

There is no question that the death of Brian Head, a fifteen-year-old who loved to write poetry, was a bullycide. On March 28, 1994, in Woodstock, Georgia, Brian walked into his economics class, placed a gun to his head, announced to his classmates, "I can't take this any more," and pulled the trigger. His mother said he had been taunted and tormented by his peers for years. "A lot of times the more popular or athletic kids would make him a target. They would slap Brian in the back of the head or push him into a locker. It just broke him." The poem Brian wrote before his death, found by his parents after his funeral, attests to the violence done to him. He writes of being seen by his peers "as an insignificant 'thing', something to be traded, mangled, and mocked". He would choose to retreat into the darkness of death because "[i]n the shadows, their evil eyes cannot stare my soul into oblivion. . . . I am free to move without their judgmental eyes on me. . . . I can sleep without dreams of despair and deception. In the shadows I am home."

Brian was a quiet, caring, and talented boy. The relentless attacks by his peers steadily broke his spirit and helped destroy his sense of self. One can only wonder how many other children choose the darkness of death over the brutality of their peers.

We do know that some kids stuff down their pain for a long time and then strike back. As many as twenty teens in an American high school of eight hundred students might be considered "high risk" for shooting others at school, according to a Harris poll underwritten by New York's Alfred University. Two thousand and seventeen students in grades seven through twelve were asked about school violence, including whether they had ever thought about shooting someone at school. Eight percent of the teens said they had thought about it, and another 10 percent said they had thought about carrying out a shooting at school. Alfred University researchers then asked about access to guns. Twenty students in every eight hundred had considered a school shooting *and* had access to a gun. Those students are most likely to be boys, in eleventh and twelfth grade, *who don't feel valued at home or at school* and who have *a perceived low quality of life*, based on their responses to the questions asked by the surveyors. Because of stricter gun controls, the gun issue is not as great in Canada, but with many ways to wreak havoc besides using guns, communities in both countries have reason to be concerned.[3]

A recent (March 8, 2001) ABC News/*Good Morning America* poll of five hundred high-school students across the nation found that when students identify a potentially violent classmate, it is generally a boy and one *who has been bullied*, rather than a bully. Seven in ten say the potential attacker they can think of is a boy; 29 percent think of both girls and boys. Just 2 percent have

---

[3] In the UK guns can only be kept under strict licence, and the much greater concern in schools is about the accessibility of knives.

only a girl in mind. Three quarters say it is more likely to be a person who is picked on than one who picks on others. Research confirms what these teenagers are saying. In a 2000 study done by the US Secret Service, in over two-thirds of the thirty-seven school shootings since 1974, the children who did the shooting all had been "persecuted, bullied, threatened, or injured".

Warning Signs for Predicting Violent Juvenile Behaviour

The following are two assessment tools listing warning signs of possible violent juvenile behaviour. These tools are intended to be used to determine if there may be a problem in the making, a tragedy brewing. They are not intended as checklists to be used for accusing a child or targeting a child for exclusion. These indicators are warning signs—red flags. It is important to be alert to both the *accumulation* and *combinations* of indicators. Some of these signs are part of the profile of "the bully", some are more descriptive of "the bullied", and some can be found in both. In my own work with young boys and girls who were troubled and/or violent, I found that they all had stories of hurt, abuse, neglect, or outright rejection. They expressed a feeling of hopelessness that was often masked by anger. They spoke of horrific injustices and violations. They came to the programme in which I was involved after they had harmed themselves or harmed others—too late for warning signs to be noticed. In retrospect, the signs were all there for anyone willing to look and listen.

The kids whose tragedies are listed in the introduction of this book all had stories containing small hints, red flags, and cries for help. But for many of them, the two lists below serve only as psychological autopsies after their deaths. Far better to use these indicators to assess the need for support and intervention before the havoc is wrought.

In his book *Protecting the Gift: Keeping Children and Teenagers Safe (And Parents Sane)*, Gavin de Becker, a leading expert on predicting violent behaviour, shares a list of preincidence indicators (PINS) that might precede teen violence:

___ 1. Alcohol and drug abuse

___ 2. Addiction to media products

___ 3. Aimlessness (constantly changing goals and ambitions, unrealistic expectations, and lack of perseverance and self-discipline to reach the goals)

___ 4. Fascination with weapons

___ 5. Experience with guns

___ 6. Access to guns

___ 7. Sullen, angry, depressed (SAD)

___ 8. Seeking status and worth through violence

___ 9. Threats (of violence or suicide)

___ 10. Chronic anger

___ 11. Rejection/humiliation

___ 12. Media provocation (widely publicized major acts of violence can stimulate people who identify with the perpetrators and the attention they receive)

He adds that many of those who commit extreme acts of violence have not learned the seven key abilities people need to effectively manage life, described by Daniel Goleman in his book, *Emotional Intelligence*:

To motivate ourselves
To persist against frustration
To delay gratification
To regulate moods
To hope
To empathize
To control impulses

The lack of any of these seven could be a preincident indicator as well. It is important to note that four of these key abilities are difficult to develop if you are the target of bullying. It's difficult to motivate yourself even to get out of bed in the morning if all you have to look forward to is a day of being bullied. It is hard to persist against frustration day in and day out when your emotional and physical well-being are under threat of attack from the moment you leave for school until you get home again; when it matters not what precautions you take or concessions you make to avoid a confrontation. It's hard to regulate moods when you are ignored, shunned, gossiped about, sneered at, and kicked. You're on a roller coaster of fear, despair, anger, frustration, and sadness. It's easier to regulate moods if you feel some sense of control over your life, when you have options available to you, and when joy, laughter, and a sense of belonging counterbalance other feelings. It's difficult to be hopeful when every day is filled with hurt and pain, rejection, and attacks. The most you can hope for is that somehow the bullying will end. If you've been bullied for a long time, you've given up any hope of anyone helping you, and you've certainly given up any hope of being able to make the bullying stop on your own.

Professor de Becker also notes that kids "at risk of committing terrible violence don't necessarily have a history of getting into trouble. . . . This means that if several preincidence indicators are present in a given boy, one's concern should not be turned into denial just because someone says, 'Oh, he's never been in trouble'." This is especially true for kids *who are the target of a bully*. When life seems intolerable, as it often does to kids who have been bullied relentlessly, only one or two indicators may signal serious trouble. Add SAD to media provocation, mix with a life that seems intolerable—thanks in large part to rejection and humiliation—and you can have a bright kid who commits suicide by flying a plane into a building.

The assessment tool for predicting violent juvenile behaviour developed by the National School Safety Center at Pepperdine University has many of the same indicators as Gavin de Becker's PINS, worded differently. Both lists include indicators omitted by the other. As parents and educators, we need all the help we can get to be aware of possible danger signs. When there is concern about the potential for violence, using indicators from both lists will not magnify the risk or blow it out of proportion. Rather, the two together can make for a clearer picture of the danger.

In the National School Safety Center's assessment tool below, a "yes" answer for each statement is assigned five points. The total score determines a child's predilection for violent behaviour.

Profile
____ Has a history of tantrums and uncontrolled outbursts.
____ Characteristically resorts to name-calling, swearing, or abusive language.

_____ Habitually makes violent threats when angry.

_____ Has brought a weapon to school.

_____ Has a background of serious disciplinary problems at school and in the community.

_____ Has a background of drug, alcohol, or other substance abuse or dependency.

_____ Is on the fringe of his peer group with few or no close friends.

_____ Is preoccupied with weapons, explosives, or other incendiary devices.

_____ Has previously been truant, suspended, or expelled from school.

_____ Displays cruelty to animals.

_____ Has little or no supervision and support from parents or a caring adult.

_____ Has witnessed or suffered abuse or neglect in the home.

_____ Bullies or intimidates peers or younger children.

_____ Tends to blame others for difficulties and problems he causes himself.

_____ Consistently prefers TV shows, movies, or music expressing violent themes and acts.

_____ Prefers reading materials dealing with violent themes, rituals, and abuse.

_____ Reflects anger, frustration, and the dark side of life in school essays or writing projects.

_____ Is involved with a gang or an antisocial group on the fringe of peer acceptance.

_____ Is often depressed and/or has significant mood swings.

_____ Has threatened or attempted suicide.

Code

5–20 points:	Youngster is potentially at risk for juvenile misbehaviour.
25–50 points:	Youngster is at risk and needs significant amount of positive support, mentoring, role modelling, and skill building.
55 points and above:	Youngster is a "ticking time bomb". The child and immediate family are at risk. Seek help from social and health services, other youth service professionals, and law enforcement.

We need to go beyond these indicators and look behind the scenes at the lives of kids who turned violent to learn how their individual makeup, their life experiences, and their environment influenced their violence. The reasons for acts of violence are as complex as the children who carry them out. Parental support, home life, peer groups, bullying, media violence, and accessibility to weapons all play some sort of role. If the assumption made by teenagers is that potential attackers in their schools are kids who were picked on—and the statistics seem to bear this out—then keeping children from becoming victims of bullying would substantially reduce the risk of future acts of violence and would certainly reduce the number of kids who, like Brian Head, chose death over facing the brutality of their peers.

Commenting on the case of Elizabeth Bush, the young girl who shot her classmate, Phillip C. McGraw, PhD, advised:

> As parents, we must take the blinders off, think the unthinkable, and see what is happening in the painful

downside of a generation that's losing its way. Acts of violence are never justifiable; but no matter how flat you make the pancake, it has two sides. The factors that led to this tragedy include acts of both commission and omission. When students reject, isolate, and psychologically torture their classmates, these children, like wounded animals, will strike back: an act of commission. They have accountability, as do those who stand idly by and allow this infliction of pain: an act of omission.

(*O* magazine, June 2001)

Those who stand idly by are part of the problem. In the next chapter we look at bystanders: who they are and how what they do (or don't do) can influence both kids who bully and kids who are bullied.

Let us not look back in anger or forward in fear, but around in awareness.

—James Thurber

CHAPTER FOUR

The Bystander

Twelve to one:
What chance had Angus? They surrounded him,
Pulled off his coat and trousers, socks and shoes,
And, wretched in his shirt, they hoisted him
Into the huge wastepaper basket; then
Poured ink and treacle on his head. With ropes
They strung the basket up among the beams
And as he soared I only saw his eyes
Look through the slats at us who watched below.

—Sir John Betjeman, *Summoned by Bells*

Bystanders are the third group of players in the story. They are the supporting cast who aid and abet the bully through acts of omission and commission. They can stand idly by or look away, or they can actively encourage the bully or join in and become one of a bunch of bullies. Whatever the choice, there is a price to pay. Actively engaging with the bully or cheering him on causes even more distress to the child who is bullied, encourages the antisocial behaviour of the bully, and puts the bystanders at risk of becoming desensitized to the cruelty or becoming fully fledged bullies themselves. When kids observe the aggressive antisocial activities of a bully, they are more likely to imitate those activities if they see the bully as a popular, strong, and daring role model. It is not uncommon for preteen boys and girls to use verbal, physical, and relational denigration of a targeted child to elevate their own status in their peer group. The apparent lack of negative consequences coupled with a bounty of prizes such as elevated status among peers, applause, laughter, and approval (or in some cases monetary rewards) for the bullying contribute to the breakdown of the bystanders' inner controls against such antisocial activities. Add to these conditions a group of peers who are caught up in this drama and you have a third ingredient: a decreased sense of individual responsibility. The bully is no longer acting alone; the bystanders have become a bunch of bullies who together denigrate the target further. This spiralling down equally reduces the guilt felt by the individual kids and magnifies the negative attributes hung on the target. "But Mum, he is such a crybaby. He whines when we just look at him." "She's such a loser; she wears such stupid clothes and walks around with her head hung down. She won't even smile."

The lack of sanctions for bullying, the breakdown of inner controls, the reduction of feelings of guilt, and the magnification of a target's negative attributes all contribute to the cultivation of a worldview that reinforces stereotypes, prejudices, and discrimination. That in turn hinders kids from developing empathy, compassion, and perspective taking (walking in another's shoes)—three essentials for successful peer relationships.

Standing idly by or turning away have their own costs. Injustice overlooked or ignored becomes a contagion that infects even those who thought they could turn away. The self-confidence and self-respect of the bystanders are eroded as they wrestle with their fears about getting involved and with the knowledge that to do nothing is to abdicate their moral responsibility to their peer who is the target.

In Sir John Betjeman's poem, Angus peered through the slats of the basket at those who watched from below. One can imagine the hopelessness and desperation in his eyes, compounded by the knowledge that those who observed his humiliation and spoke not a word of protest or raised a hand to stop it abandoned him. The cruelty was riveting to watch but distressing to contemplate. Yet contemplate it Betjeman did, over the years, before he put into words his own unease, his burden of guilt, and Angus's pain. No one is left untouched by a bullying episode.

No Innocent Bystanders

Author William Burroughs makes the provocative statement "There are no innocent bystanders" and then asks the equally provocative question, "What were they doing there in the first place?" The Bullying Circle (see illustration on next page), developed by Dan Olweus, PhD, of the University of Bergen, Norway, one of the world's leading researchers on bullying and peer harassment, indicates who these not-so-innocent bystanders are and what they are doing in a bullying situation. Starting with the bully/bullies on the left side of the circle, he names counterclockwise in order of complicity the various characters surrounding the "target—the one who is exposed":

Bully/Bullies Ⓐ
Start the bullying and take an active part

Followers/Henchmen Ⓑ
Take an active part but do not start the bullying

Supporters Passive Bully/Bullies Ⓒ
Support the bullying but do not take an active part

Passive Supporters Possible Bully/Bullies Ⓓ
Like the bullying but do not display open support

Disengaged Onlookers Ⓔ
Watch what happens; "is none of my business"; don't take a stand

Possible Defenders Ⓕ
Dislike the bullying and think they ought to help [but don't do it]

Defenders of the Target Ⓖ
Dislike the bullying and help or try to help the one who is bullied, the target

The Target Ⓨ
The one who is bullied

An adaptation of
The Bullying Circle
by Dan Olweus, PhD
Used with permission

Illustrations by Joey Coloroso

A. Bully/Bullies—who start the bullying and take an active part.
B. Followers/Henchmen—who take an active part but do not start the bullying.
C. Supporters: Passive Bully/Bullies—who support the bullying but do not take an active part.
D. Passive Supporters: Possible Bully/Bullies—who like the bullying but do not display open support.

In the middle between left and right:

E. Disengaged Onlookers—who watch what happens; say, "It is none of my business"; don't take a stand.

On the right side of the circle:

F. Possible Defenders—who dislike the bullying and think they ought to help out (but don't do it).

And the one group who are not bystanders or bullies:

G. Defenders of the Target—who dislike the bullying and help or try to help the one who is exposed—the target.

In *Olweus' Core Program Against Bullying and Antisocial Behavior: A Teacher Handbook* (Mimeo, Research Center for Health Promotion [HEMIL], University of Bergen, Norway, 1999), the author explains the usefulness of this circle as a tool for teachers, parents, and students in discussing ways to counteract and prevent bullying and the importance of kids being able and willing to move to the right side.

A 1995 Toronto, Ontario, study supported Dr Olweus's observation that the majority of peers do not come to the aid of a targeted classmate. D. J. Pepler and W. M. Craig examined the roles of peers in bullying episodes observed in urban school playgrounds. Their study revealed the following:

1. Peers were involved in some capacity in 85 percent of the bullying episodes.
2. Peers reinforced the bullying in 81 percent of the episodes.
3. Peers were more respectful and friendly toward the bullies than the targets.
4. Peers were active participants in 48 percent of the episodes.
5. Peers intervened in only 13 percent of the episodes at which they were present.

The question that begs to be asked is, Why would 81 percent of the kids who would not instigate bullying be so willing to become a part of the attack or turn a blind eye to the plight of the targeted child? There are a few valid reasons and lots of excuses.

The four reasons most often given for not intervening:

1. The bystander is afraid of getting hurt himself. The bully is bigger and stronger and has a reputation that justifies the fear; so jumping into the fray doesn't appear to be a smart thing to do.
2. The bystander is afraid of becoming a new target of the bully. Even if the bystander is able to intervene successfully, there is a chance she will be singled out at a later date for retribution. Bullies are quick to disparage

and malign anyone who tries to intervene.

3. The bystander is afraid of doing something that will only make the situation worse. In Santee, California, the friends of Andy Williams (see page xxv) were afraid that if they told administrators about Andy's threats to harm the kids who bullied him, Andy would be expelled from school. In hindsight, expulsion would have been much better than a life sentence for murder.

4. The bystander does not know what to do. He hasn't been taught ways to intervene, to report the bullying, or to help the target. Just as bullying is a learned behaviour, so must children be taught ways to stop it.

As legitimate as they are, these reasons do not shore up the self-confidence or self-respect that is eroded when a child witnesses a bullying incident and is unable or unwilling to respond effectively to stop the cruelty. All too often these fears and lack of skill can turn into apathy—a potent friend of contempt. Contempt grows best in a climate of indifference. And contempt, as we saw in Chapter Two, is what bullying is about.

Bystanders have more excuses than valid reasons for not intervening. These excuses help poison the social environment, increasing the likelihood that bystanders will side with the bully and eventually assume the role of bullies themselves. They include but are certainly not limited to these nine:

1. *The bully is my friend.* Kids are less willing to intervene when the bully is seen as a friend, even if this friend is being unfair or disrespectful.

2. *It's not my problem! This is not my fight!* Socialized not to

interfere in other people's affairs, to do their own work, and to look out for number one, bystanders can excuse themselves by claiming to be minding their own business. This is also known as indifference. In her prologue to *Rescuers: Portraits of Moral Courage in the Holocaust*, Cynthia Ozick writes of the inherent danger of such an excuse: "Indifference finally grows lethal . . . the act of turning away, however empty-handed and harmlessly, remains nevertheless an act."

3. *She is not my friend.* Kids are more willing to intervene when the targeted kid is a friend. Bullies often select kids who have few friends.

4. *He's a loser.* In a highly competitive culture it is easy to write off targets as losers. Bystanders fear they might lose their own status in their group if they are even seen with the targeted child, let alone seen defending her.

5. *He deserved to be bullied, asked for it, had it coming.* Why stop something that is warranted? He didn't even stand up for himself, so why should anyone else stand up for him? This excuse appears to get the bystander off the hook, but it fails to take into account the basic principle that bullying is about contempt. No one deserves to be stripped of his dignity and self-worth. Targeted kids cannot always act alone to successfully fend off a bully or bunch of bullies.

6. *Bullying will toughen him up.* Bullying does not toughen up a target; it humiliates and often enrages him. (See "Three Characters and a Tragedy", page 3)

7. *Kids have a deeply embedded code of silence.* Who wants to be called a snitch or a rat, blamed for getting someone else

in trouble? What isn't considered in this excuse is the immorality of silence in the face of malice.

8. *It's better to be in the in-group than to defend the outcasts.* In a clique, once the leader of the pack identifies a kid as a target, the rest of the group tends to fall mindlessly in line, doing the bully's bidding without much consideration for the rights and feelings of the outcast. The in-group becomes so tightly connected and single-minded that there is no room for protest, dissent, or differences. The need for approval and acceptance within such a clique is so strong that even if the bystander felt the momentary urge to protest the harm being done to a targeted kid, that urge would be quickly subdued. When cliques are the norm, there is a clear demarcation of "us", "them", and "kids below us and them", thus deserving of contempt and certainly not worthy of concern: "Columbine is a good, clean place except for those rejects. Most kids don't want them here."

9. *It's too big a pain in the brain.* A bystander must weigh the pros and cons of remaining faithful to the group versus siding with the targeted kid. This mental calculation can create tremendous emotional tension. The fastest way to reduce the tension is to magnify the pros of marching lockstep with the group and magnify the cons of helping out the bullied kid. Add the four legitimate reasons above to excuses number one through eight and the answer seems simple—don't get involved. Added bonus—the headache is gone. To a kid—and to many adults— standing up and speaking out can be complicated, risky, difficult, and painful.

Taken together, these reasons and excuses contribute to the erosion of civility in peer group interactions. When civility is diminished, it is replaced by a false sense of entitlement, an intolerance toward differences, and a liberty to exclude that allow kids to harm another human being without feeling empathy, compassion, or shame. This erosion of civility also erodes kids' ability to communicate, negotiate, and compromise—three vital skills necessary for solving problems, resolving conflicts, and reconciling differences peaceably.

On November 10, 2000, fourteen-year-old Dawn Marie Wesley hanged herself with her dog's leash in her bedroom. She left a note naming three girls she said were "killing her" because of bullying. In a landmark case that charts new legal territory for holding bullies to account, on Tuesday, March 26, 2002, in Abbotsford, British Columbia, one of those girls was found guilty of uttering threats, and criminal harassment. In an article in the *Globe and Mail*, Rod Mickleburgh wrote about testimony given during the trial: "They accosted the fourteen-year-old, threatening to beat her up—once in a very public location before other students. Dawn Marie was frightened and often in tears over the threats. She tried not to walk home alone. She visited the school counsellor." The provincial court judge, Jill Rounthwaite, took aim at the bystanders—those who supported Dawn Marie's tormentors, gathering around them "without recognizing that by doing so, they added to their power and intimidation. . . . I was particularly dismayed that none of the bystanders had the moral strength or the courage to stand in front of Dawn Marie Wesley and tell them to stop, go away; leave her alone." (One other girl was found not guilty of uttering threats; the third girl was found guilty of uttering threats.)

Bullying creates a climate of fear that makes kids feel unsafe. It is important that kids recognize that they are responsible for helping to create a safe, caring, respectful, and bully-free environment. The cycle of violence can be interrupted, and circles of caring can grow bigger and stronger when even one person has the moral strength and courage to stand up and speak out. When a whole community is willing to say no to the tyranny of bullies, the cycle of violence can be broken.

The Danes Take a Stand

When the Nazis (a horrifying gang of bullies) invaded Denmark in 1940, the citizens united to form a strong resistance movement. Refusing to cooperate with the planned deportation of Danish Jews, the Danes began spiriting their neighbours and relatives across the channel to Sweden in small fishing vessels. Scientists and fishermen worked together to come up with ways to numb the noses of the dogs used by the Nazis to search these vessels for stowaways. The small boats, with their undetected human cargo, met up with larger Swedish ships in the channel. In all, 7,200 of the 7,800 Danish Jews and 700 of their non-Jewish relatives were smuggled safely out of Denmark.

One of the resistance workers, Preben Munch-Nielson, wrote an account of this daring rescue. Hailing from a small Danish fishing village and only seventeen years old at the time the Jews were evacuated, he explained why he and the many other Danes defied the Gestapo:

> You can't let people in need down. You can't turn the back to people who need your help. There must be some sort of

decency in a man's life and that wouldn't have been decent to turn the back. So there's no question of why or why not. You just did. That's the way you're brought up. That's the way of tradition in my country. You help, of course . . . could you have retained your self-respect if you knew that these people would suffer and you had said, "No, not at my table?" No. No way. So that's not a problem—you just have to do it. And nothing else.

(Posted at the Holocaust Museum in Washington DC)

Just as courageous was a young German naval attaché, Georg Duckwitz, who leaked in advance to the Danes the Germans' plan for the deportation of Jews. Georg Duckwitz committed this act of conscious disobedience to save lives, willing to accept whatever penalty might be imposed as a consequence. If only some of the bystanders had been willing and able to do the same for kids like Dawn Marie.

In the next chapter, we'll explore how families can help raise decent, caring, responsible kids who can act in their own best interest, stand up for themselves, exercise their own rights while respecting the rights and legitimate needs of others, act with integrity, and have the moral strength and courage to stand up to and speak out against injustices.

> *In one way or another, as a supporter, as a perpetrator, as a victim, or one who opposed the ghastly system, something happened to our humanity. All of us South Africans were less whole. . . . Those who were privileged lost out as they became more uncaring, less compassionate, less humane, and therefore less*

human. . . . Our humanity is caught up in that of all others. We are human because we belong. We are made for community, for togetherness, for family, to exist in a delicate network of interdependence. . . . We are sisters and brothers of one another whether we like it or not, and each one of us is a precious individual.

—Archbishop Desmond Tutu,
No Future Without Forgiveness

PART TWO

Breaking the Cycle of Violence: Creating Circles of Caring

Healthy families and communities give individuals the experience of a life that extends beyond selfish interests. They are the arenas in which we learn responsibility to and for others. They provide individuals with a web of trust and social support that is desperately needed in this transient, swiftly changing society. They combat personal insecurity with a simple, ancient message: "You are not alone." When people are part of an effectively functioning community, they feel responsible in a way that isolated individuals never can.

—John W. Gardner, "National Renewal",
a speech given to the National Civic League

CHAPTER FIVE

It Runs in the Family

Our most important task as parents is raising children who will be decent, responsible, and caring people devoted to making this world a more just and compassionate place. We can fashion for ourselves and our children a warmer, kinder world that will dispel the darkness and isolation.

—Neil Kurshan,
Raising Your Child to Be a Mensch

The bully, the bullied, and the bystanders—chances are your child is involved one way or another in this daily drama. Breaking the cycle of violence that this antisocial activity creates involves recasting the roles of each of these characters, rewriting their scripts, and changing the theme of their play. Stopgap methods such as grounding, removing privileges, and spankings to punish the bully and rushing in to rescue the bullied kid provide only temporary solutions and often make matters worse. The bystanders are rarely acknowledged for their involvement or recognized as the potent force they can be to stop the bullying. The Danish activist Preben Munch-Nielson's words sum up what I think is step one in breaking the cycle of violence and creating circles of caring: "That's the way you're brought up. That's the way of tradition in my country." In *The Altruistic Personality*, Samuel and Pearl Oliner wrote that the majority of rescuers of Jews during World War II also referred to the way they were brought up and to the example of parents in explaining their actions. These heroic people were not "moral heroes, arriving at their own conclusions about right and wrong after internal struggle, guided primarily by intellect and rationality". On the contrary, "what most distinguished them were their connections with others in relationships of commitment and care". These were people who had internalized community and family norms—who talked the talk and walked the walk. When asked how long it took for them to make their decision to help, more than 70 percent said, "Minutes". Helping others was not a decision they made just in those minutes; it appeared to be a habitual response to everyday events.

How can we make acting courageously and treating others kindly, fairly, and justly habitual responses to everyday events? It is one thing to *know* what to do; it is another to actually *do* it. Moral education involves not only learning a virtue, but also knowing what constitutes virtuous behaviour and having the strength to act accordingly. A kid must *want* to be the kind of person who acts courageously—or kindly, or fairly, or justly— must know *how* to do it, and must be *willing* to do it. We can teach kids the *how*, but unless they believe that they are decent, caring, and responsible human beings, the *want* and the *will* won't be there.

The strength of our children's "connections with others in relationships of commitment and care" is determined in part by the kind of family they grow up in. The school and community also play an important role, but home is where kids get the first lessons of their moral education.

THE BACKBONE FAMILY

For children to develop their innate ability to care and their desire and will to do good, they need the support and structure of what I like to describe as a "backbone" family. What such families give their children is as strong as a firm and upright backbone, helping children develop inner discipline, so that, even in the face of adversity and peer pressure, they retain faith in themselves and in their ability to make a difference.

Backbone families are characterized not so much by what they do or don't do specifically as by how they balance the sense of self and the sense of community in all that they do. Interdependence is celebrated. There is no cycle of violence here, only an ever growing circle of caring.

Backbone families are not hierarchical, bureaucratic, or violent. Backbone parents don't demand respect—they demonstrate and teach it. Children learn to question and challenge authority that is not life-giving. They learn that they can say no, that they can listen and be listened to, that they can be respectful and be respected themselves. Children of backbone families learn to love themselves and have empathy for others. By being treated with compassion, they learn to be compassionate toward others, to recognize others' suffering, and to be willing to help relieve it. The backbone family provides the consistency, firmness, and fairness as well as the calm and peaceful structure needed for children to flesh out their own moral code. Rather than being subjected to power expressed as control and in return attempting to control others or giving up and allowing others to control them, children feel empowered. With the freedom to be themselves, they have no need to control or manipulate others, hold anyone in contempt, or subjugate themselves to a bully.

The trust between parent and child that produces optimism, perseverance, and generosity cannot grow in a family where the main concern is with order, dictatorial control, unquestioning obedience, adherence to rules, and a strict hierarchy of power. In such a family, kids are controlled and manipulated. Sometimes the techniques are obvious, blunt control tools. ("You will obey me or else." "You do what I tell you to do.") Often the techniques are subtle, though no less damaging. ("Move over, let me show you the right way to do it." "Can't you do anything right?") Children learn to do what they are told to do without questioning the person making the request or demand or questioning the purpose or consequences of the deed. Bullies learn to "boss" others around, vulnerable kids learn to "take it", and bystanders learn to "follow the leader" and assume they are powerless to change the status quo. Their feelings are often ignored, ridiculed or negated. Parents direct, supervise, minilecture, order, threaten, remind, and worry over the kids. Power in the family equals control, and all of it comes from the top. It can be a great training ground for the child who would become a bully or the proving ground for the bullied child to affirm her own lack of worth, lack of ability, and lack of personal resources to fend off the bully.

Equally damaging is a family where a permissive, laissez-faire atmosphere prevails, or where discipline is lax and there is a lack of consistency and structure. Children might one minute be smothered with attention and the next abandoned, ignored, or humiliated. They become obnoxious and spoiled and/or scared and vindictive. They don't receive the many affirming life messages that enable kids raised in a backbone family to view themselves and the world around them with optimism. (Kids who are optimistic view setbacks, mistakes, and negative social interactions as things they can control or at least do something about, rather than be immobilized and victimized by them. They are more apt to look for ways to solve problems than to place blame or give up.)

Perhaps a parent, because of her own upbringing, doesn't know how to create a healthy structure, consistency, and safe boundaries for her children. She might be frightened of repeating the abuse she knew but not know what to put in its place. She becomes extremely lax in discipline, sets few or no limits, and tends to smother her children. Since her own needs were never honoured, she has trouble recognizing them in herself and thus confuses her children's needs with her own unfulfilled needs. She has difficulty distinguishing between what her children really *need* and what they might *want*—sometimes substituting lavish gifts for spending meaningful and necessary time with her kids. Such a parent tends to become enmeshed in her children's lives, always there to smooth out problems and rescue them from any adversity, but to little effect. Research has shown that kids who are dependent on their parents to get them out of any and every situation, or who are regularly rescued by them, are more vulnerable to the antics of a bully and more willing to give in to his demands. When a parent rushes to take care of a bullying situation for her child, she not only bolsters the bully, but also sends a clear message to her child that she believes he does not have the ability to assert himself. (By no means am I implying here that an adult should never intervene. In fact, if adults see or hear of a bullying problem, they must intervene. It is the *way* the parent intervenes that makes the difference.)

The following are fifteen characteristics of a backbone family:

1. *Parents develop for their children a network of support through six critical life messages given every day:*

   - *I believe in you.*
   - *I trust you.*
   - *I know you can handle life situations.*
   - *You are listened to.*
   - *You are cared for.*
   - *You are very important to me.*

Through love, acceptance, and encouragement, children in backbone families are recognized, valued, and esteemed. They are able to fend off the verbal attacks of a bully, believe they are capable of responding assertively in a variety of confrontations, and are willing to ask for help when they don't know what to do. They know they will be listened to when they need to be heard. Nothing they say or do will be taken lightly, dismissed, or shamed.

Kids who receive these six critical life messages daily are able to develop a healthy, secure attachment with a parent. This attachment allows children to further develop their own innate abilities to be optimistic, to persevere, and to be generous. Optimism—the attitude of someone who feels positive and confident—is critical to dealing effectively with setbacks, mistakes, and negative social interactions. Optimistic kids view setbacks, mistakes, and negative social interactions as situations they can control or at least do something about, rather than be immobilized and victimized by them. They are more apt to look for ways to solve problems than to place blame or give up. Perseverance—steady and continued action or belief over long periods despite difficulties or setbacks—increases kids' confidence and gives them the strength to take risks to help others. Generosity—willingness to give help or time freely—enables kids to go beyond themselves and lose preoccupation with their own needs and wants. The development of these three innate abilities helps kids mitigate and modulate innate aggressive tendencies and helps nurture kids' empathy for their peers.

2. *Democracy is learned through experience.* At family meetings, either formal or informal, all family members are aware of events, schedules, and problems and are invited to participate as fully as possible in planning activities, fixing schedule problems, and resolving conflicts. Children see that their feelings and ideas are respected and accepted and that it is not always easy to juggle the needs and wants of all members of the family. As the children grow in responsibility and decision-making abilities, their opportunities for both are increased. Family meetings help children see their own needs and wants in relationship to others'. They become aware of what it takes to work together as a group, honour differences, and resolve conflicts peacefully.

In a family where children are not allowed to express their opinions and feelings, some children seek out others to control as they were controlled; others store up their rage and resentment and let it all loose in acts of violence against themselves or their peers; some become compliant and apathetic, easily led, manipulated, or dominated by any authority figure—including the town bully; and still others become so weakened that they have no inner resources to defend themselves against a bully or to seek help. When feelings, thoughts, and preferences are ignored, ridiculed, or punished, kids can also come to believe that there is something profoundly wrong with them, and they begin to act as if that is true, which can make them a vulnerable target for a bully. ("He's such a wimp." Could it be that he has learned to be passive to avoid his parents' wrath? "Why does she just stand there and take it?" Could it be that she has heard these same comments directed at her at home? For a vulnerable target, the negative messages the bully dishes out are reruns of what she has heard at home.)

But kids have to learn how to identify and express their feelings responsibly. If a child is neglected, his feelings disregarded, he learns to put aside or bury feelings of fear, hurt, sorrow, and anger. He learns not to trust others and to manipulate them to get what he needs. One abandoned or neglected child puts himself up by putting others down; he feels good by making others feel bad. He coolly and swiftly disposes of anyone who gets in the way of his getting what he wants. Another who is abandoned or neglected becomes absolutely self-sufficient, allowing no one to get close to her. Still another becomes so needy, constantly seeking others to make him feel safe, loved, and secure, that he becomes a prime candidate for the role of henchman for a bully.

3. *An environment is created that is conducive to creative, constructive, and responsible activity.* The physical, emotional, and moral environment in a backbone family is not rigid or unbending, nor is it cluttered with mixed messages or poor role models. Prosocial behaviours are modelled and taught. Children are encouraged to explore, play, take healthy risks, and resolve conflicts assertively and peacefully. Mistakes are viewed as opportunities to learn and grow, not as reasons for rebuke. When a child makes a mistake, is mischievous, or creates mayhem she should be held accountable every time. If sometimes an excuse is made ("I'm going to pretend I didn't see you hit him. I told you you would have to go to time-out if you hit him; next time you will", the inconsistency interferes with the child's developing a strong sense of responsibility for her own actions

4. *Discipline is handled with authority that gives life to children's learning.* When kids create mischief or act irresponsibly, they are shown what they have done wrong, are given ownership of the problem, and are offered ways to solve the problem. Their dignity is left intact. The goal of the parent is to help children develop their own self-discipline—inner discipline that enables them to be decent, responsible, caring people.

A recognized structure to the family's day-to-day life (mealtime, bedtime, chores, and recreation) is essential for maintaining discipline. Lack of structure results in absolute chaos and major problems develop. In frustration or panic, a parent may revert to the only parenting techniques she knows—threats, bribes, and punishments: "That's it. I've had it. All of you to your rooms. If you are going to fight at the table, you don't need supper." In calmer moments, there are lots of apologies and attempts to assuage the guilt the parent feels for acting just like her own parents: "I'm sorry I didn't let you eat last night. I'll take you to any restaurant you want." When the parent vacillates in this way, the children are left so disoriented and confused that they easily lose any sense of who they are and what they are capable of doing. They often seek comfort, support, and recognition from anyone— including cults and gangs of bullies—willing to give them a sense of belonging and some kind of security and consistency.

When parents employ sarcasm, ridicule, and embarrassment to manipulate and control behaviour, the results can be disastrous. ("How could you be so stupid?" "You're such a cry baby. No wonder no one will play with you." "If you are going to act like a girl, you are going to dress like one.") Bullies learn to use these tongue-lashing and name-calling tools to manipulate and control the behaviour of both the bullied child and the bystanders.

5. *Rules are simply and clearly stated.* In establishing the rules, parents draw on their own wisdom, sense of responsibility, and perception of their children's needs, constantly increasing opportunities for their children to make their own age-appropriate decisions, assume age-appropriate

responsibilities, and learn to set their own emotional, physical, moral, and ethical boundaries. ("If you want to ride your bike, you must wear a helmet. You can decide which bike helmet you would like to buy." "It's your job to walk the dog this week." "You can dislike what that boy does; it does not give you the right to call him ugly and hurtful names." See consequences below.)

6. *Consequences for irresponsible behaviour are either natural or reasonable.* They are also simple, valuable, and purposeful. There is no need for threats, bribes, or punishment. ("You will need to replace your friend's jacket that you borrowed and lost" [reasonable, simple, valuable, and purposeful]. "You hurt that boy in your class. You need to fix what you did, figure out how you are going to keep it from happening again, and find a way to heal with him. And let's look at a decent and respectful way you can tell him what he is doing that is annoying you" [reasonable, simple, valuable, and purposeful].)

Bribes and rewards and their flip side, threats and punishment, stunt the child's ability to make a choice. "If you share your toys with your brother, you can pick a treat at the grocery store" (bribe). "You will share your toys with your brother or you will spend the rest of the afternoon in your room" (threat). "You can pick out a toy in the store since you shared a toy with your brother" (reward). "I'm locking up all of your toys since you obviously can't share with your brother" (punishment). None of these provides an opportunity for a child to willingly choose to share. All seem to demonstrate that we are operating from an attitude of fear rather than faith. If we don't give our child a reward for sharing, we worry, "Will she ever learn to share? Will she continue to share if we don't reward her each time she shares? Will we create a selfish brat if we don't try to entice her to share or punish her for refusing to share?" External motivation merely manipulates a child into performing a specific task. It does not inspire anyone to be tolerant, compassionate, honest, trustworthy, or fair. Even when bribes and threats appear to work, children who "do to please" have no deep understanding of the deeds they have done, they often have little or no commitment to what they are doing, and most important, they fail to gain genuine concern for their siblings or peers. Deeds are done merely or mostly for the payoff. Children who "do to please" can easily become overly dependent on others for approval and recognition, lacking self-confidence and a sense of responsibility—ideal traits for a bystander who willingly joins with the bully or stands on the sidelines.

Physical punishment is easy and swift and may stop the misbehaviour immediately. But if our goal is to develop inner discipline—that is, discipline motivated by inner rather than outer controls—it fails miserably. Not doing something because you might get hit is not the same as not doing something because it is wrong to do. Research has shown that the majority of bullies and kids who readily succumb to the bullying come from homes where harsh physical punishment is used consistently (or used randomly and arbitrarily). Punishment increases anger and aggression and greatly inhibits the development of empathy. Hitting children demonstrates to them that it's all right for people to hit people—especially for bigger people to hit smaller people or stronger people to hit weaker people. The bully is likely to take this technique to school and victimize smaller or weaker peers. Targeted kids who succumb to the bullying often lack inner resources to fend off the bully—having had these resources (a strong sense of self and an ability to respond assertively) quite literally beaten out of them.

7. *Children get second opportunities.* Kids are clearly given responsibility and a reasonable consequence for not following through. When they blow it—and kids will—they are given a second opportunity to try again, *after* they have experienced the consequences for blowing it the first time. By being held accountable for what they do and being able to fix the problems they create, they are less likely to place blame for their behaviour outside of themselves and onto their peers.

8. *Children are motivated to be all they can be.* They are accepted as they are and invited and encouraged to be more than they thought they could be. Learning takes place in an atmosphere of acceptance and high expectation. ("I know Jill's behaviour bothers some of your friends. But it is not right to invite everyone else in the group to your sleepover and exclude her. I know you can figure out how to make your sleepover party work. I'm here to help if you need it.") They are held to high standards of conduct not to please their parents, but because their parents believe they are capable of being decent, responsible, caring people. They are taught to act with civility—that is, to treat someone with the same

dignity and respect they would want for themselves, even if they don't actually like that person—to be willing when necessary to set aside their own wants and concerns for the larger good, to criticize, to hold accountable (but always with regard for the humanity of the other person), and to resolve differences respectfully.

9. *Children receive lots of smiles, hugs, and humour.* All three are given freely and without conditions attached. Children learn that touch is critical to human bonding by watching parents give affection to each other and by receiving loving and caring touches themselves. They see their parents enjoying life and sharing laughter *with* them, not laughing *at* them. They are less likely to laugh at their peers if they themselves are not the butt of someone's joke at home.

10. *Children learn to accept their own feelings and to act responsibly on those feelings through a strong sense of self-awareness.* Parents are empathic and emotionally available to them, modelling appropriate ways to express the full range of emotions. ("I am sad that he is moving to a new town. I will miss him." "It's okay to cry, son. I am sad, too, that their family won't be our neighbours any more. You and Sam had many wonderful times together. Let's think of something to do that will make the move a little easier for him." "I am so angry at Sara. She told everyone I was a slut." "Susan, it's okay to be angry with Sara; what she did was cruel. Let's look at what you can do with your anger that would be constructive, and think of what steps you can take to confront her.") Kids learn to acknowledge and honour their own feelings. They also learn that they don't need to act on every emotion they have. Their own

empathy is nourished, perspective taking is developed, and acts of compassion are encouraged. When their feelings are recognized and validated by their parents, children are less likely to become enmeshed in the feelings of their peers. Critical to responding to peers empathetically is the ability of children to see their own feelings as separate from those of their peers and to respond to the sadness, fear, or hurt without becoming so sad, fearful, or hurt that they themselves are overcome or immobilized. They are able to see the pain, know what that feeling is like, and respond in a way that will relieve that pain.

When parents demand obedience and rule by fear, kids are taught at a very young age not to express their true feelings. Spontaneous expressions of joy, concern, and happiness are stifled, because *the parents stifle all feelings.* Eventually the child becomes so wary of her parents that *no* feelings are expressed spontaneously; she must first "check in" with her parents to see if the feeling is okay. Feelings of anger, fear, sadness, or hurt are not just stifled, they are directly punished or denied. Forbidden to express these emotions themselves, kids get stuck in their anger, fear, sadness, and hurt. Sometimes they even refuse to acknowledge that they are angry or hurt and have no way of getting rid of the energy produced by those feelings. The energy builds up inside, like steam pressure in a boiler. Eventually one of three things results:

a. Passive-destructive acts against the self. These acts signal poor self-esteem or even self-hatred. A passive-destructive person often avoids dealing openly with feelings or blames others for "causing" them. "I'm not sad." "It didn't hurt." "It's his fault." Instead of solving the problem, these acts negatively impact the person who has the problem.

b. Aggressive acts against others. An aggressive person tries to control others with verbal, physical, or relational bullying. These acts don't solve the original problems. Instead they create new ones.

c. Passive-aggressive acts (a combination of the other two). These acts combine the first two in a creative way that signals that the person is responsible neither for himself nor to others. She doesn't deal with people or issues directly, but uses devious ways to hurt them, making sarcastic remarks or put-downs and declaring she was just kidding, spreading rumours or pretending to care while in reality intending to harm. She harbours her anger and uses the negative energy to attack targets who may be more popular, pretty, smarter, or kinder.

11. *Competency and cooperation are modelled and encouraged.* Parents demonstrate the ability to do a variety of tasks, and they help their children learn new skills. They show their children how to work and play with others. They show them how to become competent, cooperative, and decisive. ("Let's figure out a bike trip for this weekend. I'll check the bikes this time. Who wants to fill the water bottles, make the snacks, or map out the bike path route? Let's think of someone we can include to ride our extra bike." "We're inviting the new neighbours over for dinner,

because that's what you do when new people move in."
"When a new kid comes to class, what can you do to help
him feel included?" "What can you do if your friends don't
want him to eat at your lunch table?")

Competition is recognized as a reality in their lives, but
kids are taught to celebrate their own success *and* to
acknowledge the empathy they feel for those who lose. The
dark side of competition is that it can negatively affect
kids' feelings toward their siblings and peers, stifling the
development of this empathy. Rather than celebrate
diversity and honour differences, heavy reliance on
competition trains kids to see others as obstacles to their
own success or as adversaries. It also separates kids into
winners and losers. If the bully is seen as a winner (who
won at the expense of the dignity and self-worth of the
targeted child), bystanders are more likely to side with the
winner and not want to be seen with the loser, let alone
come to his aid.

12. *Love is unconditional.* Because they are children and for no
other reason, they have dignity and worth—simply
because they are. ("I love you." "You are fun to be with."
"I'm here if you need me.") Kids who feel loved, wanted,
and respected are more willing to celebrate differences and
welcome others into their circle of caring.

When love is conditional, it is not really love at all. Kids
who must constantly earn their parents' approval are so
busy "doing to please" that they don't have the time or
energy to figure out who they are and what unique gifts
they bring to life. They depend on others to affirm their
worthiness or unworthiness. They are willing to do

whatever is asked of them by a dominant peer to get his or her affection and approval.

Since they feel unworthy, they may see others as just as unworthy and may feel no qualms about hurting others, reasoning, "If I have no worth, neither do they." Or, having no way to deflect an attack, they may be so vulnerable that a bully's verbal abuse cuts to the core of their being. They are willing to do whatever is asked of them by a dominant peer to get his or her affection and approval or to make the bullying stop.

13. *Children are taught how to think.* They are encouraged to listen to their own intuition, to be spontaneous, to be creative in thoughts and actions, and to reason through problems. They are spoken with, not to; listened to, not ignored. They are encouraged to challenge authority that is not life-giving, as well as to respect the true wisdom of their elders. They are given a thirst for knowledge of the old and a spirit of curiosity to discover the new. ("When you have a gut feeling about something, trust your own intuition." "You'll figure out a way to solve that problem; I know you can do it." "Can you tell me how you feel about it and what you think we can do to fix it?" "I hear what you are saying. I hadn't thought of it that way." "If someone in a position of authority asks you to do something that is unkind, unjust, unfair, hurtful, or dishonest, you need to listen to your own conscience." "You can stand up and speak out when you see an injustice being committed. If one of your classmates is bullying another child, there are several ways you can be helpful in stopping the bullying. Let me show you some of them.")

Children are taught to figure out a good course of action when facing a moral dilemma. They are able to bring together objective "rightness" (what to think) and subjective "discernment" (how to think) to figure out what could be a good course of action to end a bullying situation. Then the "what to think" and "how to think" are used to connect actions (What can I do?), intentions (Why am I doing it?), and the circumstances of a situation (to whom, when, where, how, potential intended and unintended consequences, and possible alternatives). This course of action becomes a way of life for them.

If children are taught what to think, they are more easily manipulated and more likely to do something to please someone else rather than do what may be good for them or for someone in need. ("Why don't you wear the red dress? You look better in it than that blue one." "Don't you think you should wear a coat?" "Don't play with him. He's not our kind.") If children are told what to think and not taught how to reason through a problem nor allowed to make their own choices and decisions within reasonable limits and with adult guidance, they will be unable to "think outside the box" to come up with viable alternatives to bullying someone else to get their own needs met or to succumbing to a bully, or to summon the inner resources required to intervene effectively on behalf of a bullied peer.

14. *Children are buffered from the possible impact of a bully, or from the need to become a bully, by the daily reinforcement of the messages that foster a strong sense of self:*

- **I like myself.** Kids know they are loved
  unconditionally, and are capable of taking full
  responsibility for their own thoughts and actions.
  When a bully taunts them, they can do positive self-
  talk: "I am a good and capable and compassionate
  human being. That kid who is calling me names is
  mistaken, having a bad day, and/or trying to get her
  own needs met in a mean way."
- **I can think for myself.** Kids who can think for
  themselves are less likely to be manipulated by a peer
  or go along with the crowd. Given lots of
  opportunities to make choices and decisions with
  adult guidance, not adult directives, they are able to
  step in when everyone else is stepping away, to speak
  up when everyone else falls silent, and to withstand
  criticism for their actions.
- **There is no problem so great it can't be solved.** Kids
  who are encouraged to solve problems tend to be
  competent and resilient in the face of adversity.
  Realities are accepted. Problems are solved. "You have
  a classmate who is bullying others" (reality). "Let's
  look at some ways you can help the child who is being
  bullied" (problem to solve). "You said the bully
  seemed to be all alone. Maybe not too many people
  have been nice to him. Do you think you could invite
  him to join the rest of you at the lunch table?"
  (problem to solve). "That was a hurtful thing to say to
  her" (reality). "We need to talk about what would
  make you want to put someone else down so cruelly"
  (problem). "What do you think you can do to make

proper amends?" (problem to solve). "I will follow up with you to talk about how it turned out."

15. *The family is willing to seek help.* Problems are not denied or hidden. Parents recognize when they need to seek advice from elders or trained professionals and receive the advice with an open mind and heart. ("Our son is bullying other children. What can we do to help him change his behaviour and his heart?" "My daughter is having trouble standing up to her classmate who likes to hurt younger kids in the playground." "My son is a target of the town bully. What can we do to help him and to stop the violence?")

Being a backbone parent isn't easy. There are no quick fixes, no sure answers, just lots of opportunities to grow. If you aren't already one, *becoming* a backbone parent is even more difficult. Remember that you cannot change everything overnight. You might need help and support to make the changes that will be necessary. You might be able to find that help in a supportive neighbour, friend, or mentor. Sometimes a family therapist or counsellor can help you make sense of where you have been, where you are going, and what you can do to get there. If you are currently punishing or rescuing your children, you can change your attitudes, behaviours, and habits. In turn, you will change your relationship with your children, which will in turn affect the way they relate to their siblings and peers.

If we want to influence and empower our children to break the cycle of violence, our daily behaviour needs to flow from that belief. If we make disparaging comments about people in our community, we are teaching our children intolerance, bigotry, and hatred. If in our words and actions we demonstrate tolerance, acceptance, kindness, and compassion, our children will tend to do the same. If our children witness us standing up for values we believe in and speaking out against injustices, they are more likely to transfer those lessons to their own everyday experiences than if we tell them they must never bully or make them "share" with their sister "or else."

Growing up in a hostile, cold, and punitive household will not eliminate the possibility of a child becoming a decent, caring, responsible person; however, such an environment will significantly reduce the chances of it happening. In creating a warm, caring, nurturing environment for our children, we get no guarantee that they will become decent, caring responsible people, but in such an environment the possibility becomes much more likely.

> *When a family is free of abuse and oppression, it can be the place where we share our deepest secrets and stand the most exposed, a place where we learn to feel distinct without being "better" and sacrifice for others without losing ourselves.*
>
> —Letty Cottin Pogrebin,
> *Family Politics*

CHAPTER SIX

Is There a Bully in the House?

When people have learned to desanctify each other, to treat each other as means to our own ends, to not feel the pain of those who are suffering, we end up creating a world in which these terrible acts of violence become more common. . . . I categorically reject any notion that violence is ever justified. It is always an act of desanctification, not being able to see the divine in the other.

—Rabbi Michael Lerner,
"Our Estrangement From God",
From the Ashes

None of us wants to think that our child is bullying other kids. But if you are worried that your child might be a bully, you can stop worrying and look carefully at the clues that give you cause to be concerned. It is important to remember that bullying is not about anger or conflict; it's about contempt—a powerful feeling of dislike toward somebody considered to be worthless, inferior, and undeserving of respect. Rabbi Lerner calls it "desanctification, not being able to see the divine in the other". Pierre Teilhard de Chardin called it "dehumanization", not being able to see the humanity in the other person. No matter what it's called, it is easy for you to check to see whether the behaviour that is causing you concern has the four markers of bullying: imbalance of power, intent to harm, threat of further aggression, and terror. Along with those four markers, you may sense in your child an attitude of entitlement to control, dominate, subjugate, or otherwise abuse another person; an intolerance toward differences; and a mistaken assumption that he or she has the liberty to exclude someone not deemed worthy of respect or care. The punch your son gave his playmate was not born of anger or frustration; it came from calculated aggression. He seemed to have no empathy, compassion, or shame. In fact, he displayed an air of indifference as he calmly explained to you that his playmate was a big crybaby. Your daughter held her younger brother's arm behind his back and twisted it until he screamed in pain. The look on her face seemed to be one of pleasure. Seeing you come into the room, she quickly grabbed her brother and tried to soothe his pain. But you saw that cold smile before your daughter saw you. The teacher called to say your son and a group of his friends circled a young boy in the school cafeteria, squirting him with ketchup and calling him "fag". No, it was not playful teasing, and yes, it was your son who seemed to be leading the pack. While driving the school run, you overheard your daughter and friends laughing about the ugly prank they pulled on the new kid. Your son referred to the new girl in school as if she were a prime cut of meat. You are stunned. He says that's the way all the kids talk; where have you been?

Terrorizing, intimidating, shunning, tormenting, and

ridiculing are not sibling rivalry or peer conflicts. They are acts of bullying. It is important that you not make light of what happened and write it off as "usual stuff" between siblings or playmates. It is just as important that you not try to justify, rationalize, or minimize. "The other boy was aggravating my son." "The girls were just playing around. They didn't mean to hurt the new kid." "Everyone gets teased." Letting your child get away with such behaviour does not serve her well. You are subtly saying that you don't expect much more from her, thus giving her a ready-made excuse for being cruel or violent.

It is also important that you not punish your child. Punishing your child will only teach him to be more aggressive and hurtful. He will undoubtedly master the art of doing his bullying in ways that are sneaky or "under the radar" of even the most observant and aware adults. More important, punishment degrades, humiliates, and dehumanizes the children who are its objects. (Sounds like bullying to me.) Punishment is preoccupied with blame and pain. It does not consider reasons or look for solutions. It pre-empts more constructive ways of relating to a child. It drives people further apart, and it enables the parent and child to avoid dealing with the underlying causes of the bullying. The overriding concerns of punishment are: What rule was broken? Who did it? and What kind of punishment does the child deserve? Punishment deprives the child of the opportunity to understand the consequences of her actions, to fix what she has done, or to empathize with the child she has harmed.

Studies of the background of bullies and their most vulnerable targets conclude that physical punishment (and/or neglect) played a big role in the lives of both. What has not been researched is the part more subtle forms of punishment play. I suspect that these have a negative impact as well. Following are the most common:

- Isolation ("If you twist his arm again, you will stay in your room for the rest of the day.")
- Embarrassment and humiliation ("If you are going to act like a one-year-old, you will have to dress like one as well. Go get me a nappy.")
- Shaming ("Shame on you for hurting him.")
- Emotional isolation ("Don't come to me for a hug—you were a bad girl to hurt your brother.")
- Grounding ("You can't go over to your friend's house, watch TV, or use the phone until you learn to treat your brother better.")

Note how these subtle forms of punishment resemble relational and verbal bullying. Embarrassment, humiliation, and shaming might make a parent feel good about doing something besides physically punishing, but they are unlikely to change the behaviour of the bully. He will probably avoid taking responsibility for the wrongdoing, concentrating more on how badly he is being treated than on what he did that initiated the punishment. With both these and physical punishment, children are robbed of the opportunity to develop their own inner discipline—the ability to act with integrity, wisdom, compassion, and mercy when there is no external accountability for what they do.

Can a child feel ashamed of what he has done? Yes, but he can't be shamed into feeling ashamed or guilty or remorseful. Those feelings must come from the inside, not from the outside. It is okay—in fact, it is important—to feel guilty about something done intentionally to harm someone else. That's what having a conscience is all about. But the feeling of guilt won't be there unless the feeling of empathy has been cultivated. Empathy and guilt go hand in hand. Your son must care about others' feelings and be able to "walk in their shoes" before he can feel guilty about hurting them or treating them unfairly. Your role is not to shame him, it is to let him know that what he did was wrong and that you care enough about him to help him make it right. When you care this much about your son, he will be more ready to transfer this caring to others. Activist and author Carl Upchurch explained how important this caring is to empathic connection: "I think that they matter because you think that I matter."

If you know your child is bullying his siblings or peers, you will need to act immediately and decisively. Consider your own behaviour. Is there anything you are doing to encourage or support the bullying? If the answer is yes, as discussed in the last chapter, you can change your attitudes, behaviours, and habits. In turn, you will change your relationship with your child, which in turn will affect the way he relates to his peers and siblings.

If the answer is no, there could be other socializing influences that are giving rise to your child's bullying—peer relationships or social and educational environments such as day care and school. Since bullying is about contempt, excuses such as emotional, physical, or mental handicaps are just that—excuses. Bullying is a purposeful, thought-out activity intended to harm someone who is seen as inferior or unworthy of respect and concern. Being hyperactive, having an attention deficit, or showing signs of neurological damage may contribute to a child's aggressive behaviour, but they do not "cause" a child to have disregard, loathing, or hate for someone else. Those states of mind and heart have to be learned.

Whether the answer is yes or no, know that you can do something to stop the bullying. In his book, *Parents Under Siege*, Professor James Garbarino reminds us that as parents "we are *responsible* for our children's actions; we are not necessarily to *blame* for them." It is good if you can stop the bullying in the early stages before the lines of the role are mastered and your child is typecast as the bully. But it is never too late to change the dynamics. Just as your child was capable of being disrespectful and malicious and callous, so is he capable of being respectful, kind, and compassionate. He learned to bully; he can learn more prosocial ways to act with his peers. The list of traits bullies have in common on page 21 can be summed up in what bullies are not good at: caring about others, being kind to siblings or peers, sharing, getting along, and making friends. Helping your child develop these skills will go a long way toward helping your child take on a new, more constructive role. There needs to be a change in both your child's thinking and behaviour.

There are things you can do:

1. Intervene immediately with discipline.
2. Create opportunities to "do good".
3. Nurture empathy.
4. Teach friendship skills—assertive, respectful, and peaceful ways to relate to others.
5. Closely monitor your child's TV viewing, video game playing, computer activities, and music.
6. Engage in more constructive, entertaining, and energizing activities.
7. Teach your child to "will good".

1. Intervene immediately with discipline.

Discipline is not judgmental, arbitrary, confusing, or coercive. It is not something we *do to* children. It is a process that gives life to learning; it is restorative and invites reconciliation. Its goal is to instruct, teach, guide, and help children develop self-discipline—an ordering of the self from the inside, not imposition from the outside. In disciplining a child who has bullied someone, we are concerned not with mere compliance ("Don't bully, say you're sorry, and then just leave him alone"), but with inviting him to delve deeply into himself and reach beyond what is required or expected. When a child has developed his own moral code, committed himself to acting kindly and justly, believes he has both the ability to control his behaviour and a choice in how he behaves, and takes responsibility for his own actions, he will be able to get his own needs met while treating others with the same dignity and regard with which he would like to be treated.

Discipline provides the tools necessary to begin the healing process when serious material or personal harm has occurred. It deals with the reality of the situation, not the power and control of the adult. It helps change attitudes and habits that led to the bullying and promotes genuine peace in the home.

The process of discipline has four steps that the act of punishment does not have:

1. It shows the bully what he has done wrong—no mincing words, soft-pedalling it as a conflict, or minimizing the activity. ("Gee, everybody calls people names in the lunchroom.")
2. It gives him ownership of the problem—no excuses ("We

didn't mean to hurt him; we were only teasing"), no blame shifting ("James started it; I didn't"), no buts ("But he is such a loser"), no if onlys ("If only he wouldn't act like that, then we wouldn't bother him").

3. It gives him a process for solving the problem he created—restitution, resolution, and reconciliation; in other words, he must fix what he did, figure out how to keep it from happening again, and heal with the person he has harmed.

4. It leaves his dignity intact—he is not a bad person; what he did was despicable; we believe he is capable of being a decent, caring, responsible kid.

Discipline is a constructive and compassionate response to bullying that takes into consideration the intent, the severity of the deed, and the restorative steps needed to help the bully take on a new, more prosocial role. It will involve your time as well as your child's time. However, the time you take is well worth it as your child begins to realize that all of his actions have intended and unintended consequences. He will learn that he is quite capable of taking responsibility and ownership for what he did and just as capable of taking full responsibility for the harm he caused, not because he fears reprisal, but because it is the right thing to do.

ARM-TWISTING AND DISCIPLINE

When you walked in on your daughter twisting her brother's arm, twisting her arm in turn to teach her a lesson, isolating her, embarrassing her, shaming her, telling her you don't love little girls who are mean to their brother, or grounding her won't teach her to not harm her brother; rather, it will teach her to do it in a way that she won't get caught next time. Punishment will likely enable her to see herself as a victim of your punishment rather than as the agent of her brother's pain. Dismissing it or hoping it was a passing aberration will invite your daughter to bully even more. The constructive alternative is the four steps of discipline, with the three Rs—restitution, resolution, and reconciliation—being an integral part of the third step.

You can clearly state what she did and affirm your belief that she is capable of fixing the mess she made. "You twisted your brother's arm. You hurt him and you need to make amends for this hurt. I'll walk through the three Rs with you. I know you can handle this."

The first R, restitution, means fixing what she did. Had she broken her brother's favourite toy, she would have needed to fix or replace that toy. Material damage is usually easier to repair than personal damage. The pain felt by her brother, the fear he may have of his sister hurting him again, and his lack of trust that she will treat him kindly are harder to fix than putting together the pieces of a broken toy.

An apology is in order, but it is requested, not demanded. If you demand an apology, you will get either an insincere "I'm sorry" or repeated insincere apologies after repeated arm-twistings. Such obligatory repentance doesn't heal any rift. A sincere apology is more likely to be forthcoming if the child has seen it modelled or has been the recipient herself of a sincere "I'm sorry".

No matter how heartfelt, just speaking the words *I'm sorry* is not enough. An elementary-school teacher explained it to her students with a vivid example. She hammered a nail into a block of soft wood. As she hit the nail repeatedly, she asked her students to think of times when they physically hurt someone, verbally taunted them, or shunned them. With the claw of the hammer, she pulled the nail out of the wood. Holding up the nail, she said, "This is the 'I'm sorry', but it's not enough." Holding up the block of wood, she asked the students, "What are we going to do about the hole the nail left in the wood?" To repent honestly and unconditionally means to assume responsibility for the deed, admit the wrongness of what has been done, express a strong desire not to do it again, assume responsibility for the damage, and begin to mend the torn relationship.

Repentance cannot be forced upon your child, but you can help her arrive at repentance by helping her work her own way through the three Rs. Repentance is not a goal in itself. Rather, it is a by-product that comes about only as she works through the whole process of reconciliation.

The second R, resolution, means figuring out a way to keep the incident from happening again. In other words, how can your daughter create herself anew—not apart from what she has done, or in spite of what she has done, or because of what she has done? Creating anew involves integrating the destructive act (twisting her brother's arm) and all its results and implications into a new beginning. It happened. She can't go back and undo the deed. Wishing it hadn't happened isn't productive, either. She needs to be able to figure out what she actually did (no, it wasn't an accident; she intended harm), what she did to bring it about (yes, she was jealous, and yes, she was angry—not at her brother, but at the fact that he never seemed to get in trouble and she seemed to always get into trouble), and what she can learn from it (I am capable of hurting someone when I feel jealous or angry, when I disregard his feelings, and when I don't try to see the situation from his point of view. I can get my own needs met in a way that doesn't hurt my brother; it's all right to be upset or angry, it is never all right to twist his arm to hurt him). It is at this point that you can talk with your daughter about being aware of the consequences of her actions—the impact her actions have on her brother (it hurts to have your arm twisted), the impact they have on her relationship with her brother (no one likes to be around people who hurt them), and the impact they have on her (twisting arms is a lousy way to play with other people; soon I will have no one who will want to play with me. I want to and can be a decent, caring, responsible kid who is fun to have as a sister). You can help your daughter work through her feelings and help her practise more prosocial behaviours (see number two below). If her actions were motivated by jealousy—disregard or contempt for a sibling is often rooted in jealousy—it is important that you examine the way you treat both kids. It is easy to cast siblings into fixed roles of the "bully" and the "bullied", with each being perceived by you and each other in those roles and acting accordingly.

The third R, reconciliation, is a process of healing with the person you have harmed. It involves a commitment by the offender to honour her plan to make restitution and live up to her resolutions. It also involves willingness on the part of her brother to trust, risk, and rebuild a relationship with her. After making restitution and coming up with practical resolutions, it is helpful if your daughter offers her time and talent to her brother. ("Your brother didn't get off to such a great start today getting his arm twisted. What can you do to help him have a better day?" "He likes to be pulled in the wagon.") Your daughter pulls your son in the wagon. This serves two purposes: one, the bullied brother can experience the goodness of his sister; and two, the bullying sister can experience her own ability to be good and do good ("I messed up. I am a decent, caring, responsible person who can fix what I did wrong, figure out how to keep it from happening again, and heal with the brother I have harmed").

Kids would most likely be inclined to stop at step two and be done with the whole ordeal. It is important that this third step take place. It is up to the adult to orchestrate it. With your daughter who has not yet become typecast in the role of bully—she's just practised it a few times—this step can happen fairly quickly and help her readily assume a more prosocial role. Her brother, who has not been the target of relentless bullying by his sister, will probably be willing to hop in the wagon and go for a ride. The cycle of violence has been halted, and a strong circle of caring is being created.

This is not the case when you are faced with a situation where the teacher calls to tell you your son has been tormenting another child relentlessly and the other child has no desire ever to be in contact with your son, let alone take part in a reconciliation, no matter how much your son expresses true remorse, tries to make restitution, and comes up with great resolutions. Too often, kids who have bullied and the kids they have bullied are forced into conflict resolution workshops—but remember, bullying is not about conflict; it is about contempt. There is no conflict to be resolved. The bully merely puts on his charm for the adults and shows the obligatory remorse—this is just another act with new lines. The bullied child gets no relief, no support, and the bully learns no genuine empathic or prosocial behaviours. There is a chance the bully will seek revenge or the target will recant his story out of fear of that revenge. The bullying will likely continue.

Your son can work on all of the above up to the point of reconciliation and then must be willing to be patient in waiting for the bullied child to be open to true reconciliation with him. Time, in and of itself, does not heal relationships, but it does take time to heal. Even if your son went to the other boy with a heartfelt apology and offer of restitution, the bullied boy might need more time to become stronger himself before he can reconcile. The *intention* behind asking for time is not to hurt your son, make him feel the same pain he inflicted, or make him suffer as much as he made the other boy suffer. The time may be needed for the target of your son's bullying to face the hurt, vent his emotions, and begin to release any grudges and destructive feelings, so that he not only reclaims his own peace of mind, sense of security and safety, and sense of well-being, but also can begin to open his heart and his hands to reconciliation with your son.

Your son can show respect by honouring the distance that may need to be kept during this waiting period. If anyone is to be inconvenienced at this point, it is to be your son. He may have to steer clear of any situation that would put the two of them together, whether it is in the hallway, in the science class, or at the soccer game. He may have to do home study if the child he bullied is too fearful to be in the same school as your son. He may have to be more closely supervized and restricted to certain areas of the playground. His actions will probably be closely monitored. Your son may balk at these conditions. You can gently remind him that it was he who did the bullying.

When the other child is ready, he and your son can come together to look for creative solutions to solving the problems that they face in order to be reconciled. This is not the same as seeing the bullying itself as a conflict. The problems that need to be solved relate to how the two can live together in the school community *after* the bullying has stopped and *after* the bully has worked through the steps of discipline.

2. Create opportunities to "do good".

It's not enough to tell your son what he cannot do; he needs to figure out what he can do. With your guidance and supervision, he can find opportunities to behave toward others in caring and helpful ways. In the process of reconciliation, he will be doing something good for someone he has harmed. What your child can do now is to practise "doing good" *before* he even thinks of harming someone else, not just after the fact. The more times he behaves toward others in caring and helpful ways, the less likely he will be to want to treat them (or anyone else) with disregard. You can brainstorm with your child ways to be helpful at home, in the neighbourhood, and at school. "Your brother is having trouble with his multiplication tables. You've got them down pat. Do you think you could help your brother learn them?" "Mrs Smith has been ill and her garden is overgrown with weeds. Do you think you could clean it up for her?" You can also invite your child to join you in doing something helpful in your community.

Giving your son chores to do, such as dumping the trash, and important responsibilities to assume, such as feeding the dog, may not sound like ways to help your child learn to "do good". Not only do these ordinary activities help children develop the ability to organize their own resources, experience closure on a task, organize their time, set goals, and build skills necessary for working through more complex tasks, they send a special message to kids: "You are an important member of our family; we need you, and we are counting on you to help out." Kids need to believe that they can make a contribution, can make a difference in their families, neighbourhood, and school. "Doing good" is a step beyond helping your child get his own needs met. It also helps your child learn to notice and care about the rights and needs of others, which in turn helps him to nurture his ability to empathize with others.

3. Nurture empathy.

Empathy is the core virtue around which all other virtues are built. In her book, *Building Moral Intelligence*, Michele Borba describes empathy as "the ability to identify with and feel another person's concerns. . . . This first moral virtue is what sensitizes our kids to different points of view and increases their awareness of others' ideas and opinions. Empathy is what enhances humanness, civility, and morality. Empathy is the emotion that alerts a child to another person's plight and stirs his conscience. It is what moves children to be tolerant and compassionate, to understand other people's needs, to care enough to help those who are hurt and troubled."

Empathy is an inborn quality in human beings. Our emotional states are influenced by the emotional states of those around us. Even newborns respond to the distress cries of other infants. By the time they are one year old, children can be observed trying to comfort someone who is sad or hurt. Still not fully able to understand the other child's feelings as being separate from their own feelings, one-year-olds try to comfort the other child by doing what would comfort themselves. They go and get their own mum, even if the other child's mother is present, or give their own favourite toy to the child in distress. By two years of age, they are capable of understanding that feelings have causes and that as toddlers they are capable of doing things to help someone feel happy or sad. By four years of age, most children can take another person's perspective—a critical milestone in being able to reflect on the impact of their own behaviour on other people and to come to the aid of someone in distress. By the time they are six or seven, children are more intellectually capable of responding constructively and more emotionally capable of responding with compassion—able to see what the other person needs to relieve his stress and able to more accurately identify with what the other person is feeling.

In his book, *Empathy and Moral Development: Implications for Caring and Justice*, Professor Martin L. Hoffman explains that at the most advanced stage of empathy, a person is able to process nonverbal and verbal messages, situational cues, and the knowledge of the other person's life condition. A person can then imagine the emotions and experiences suggested by that information and reflect on all of it. "In this way they gain understanding and respond affectively to the circumstances, feelings, and wishes of the other, while maintaining the sense that this person is separate from themselves." Such a level of empathy would prevent your son from coldly and callously harming his classmate or prevent your daughter from maliciously twisting her brother's arm. They would both be able to see other children as worthy of the same regard as they, and be able to look ahead to see what pain their actions would cause for the other children. They would also be more willing to stand up and speak out when anyone else was treating another child unfairly or unjustly.

Bullies tend to have poor perspective-taking skills, seeing

incidents only from their own point of view and being concerned only about their own feelings. The language of a bully is, "You will give me what I want; I don't care how you feel," or, "I do care how you feel: the worse, the better." If your child is bullying others, he does not lack empathy. It is still there, deep down inside him, but it is going to take time and effort to uncover it.

Your child can learn to recognize his siblings' or peers' sadness, hurt, or dejection and identify with their distress. He can also learn to imagine how it would feel if he were in their shoes and know how to extend kindness and help. You can begin to help him by sharing your own feelings, explaining why you feel the way you do, responding empathetically to him, helping him become aware of how his hurtful behaviour affects others, teaching him principled moral prohibitions against hurting others, and helping him develop his perspective-taking abilities.

Feelings and thoughts lead to action. By using everyday situations, you can teach your child to first recognize and label his feelings and identify his thoughts: "How did you feel when you failed your exam?" "How did you feel when you helped your teammate score that goal?" "How did you feel when you shoved that boy into the locker?" "How did you feel when you helped your sister?" "How did you feel when you twisted your brother's arm?" "What were your thoughts about your teammate scoring that goal?" "What thoughts did you have about the boy you shoved into the locker?" "What did you think about your ability to help your sister?"

The next step is to help him take on another person's perspective. One way to do that is to have your child walk in another's shoes, to feel what the other person felt, and to think about what the other person thought: "How do you think your teammate felt when you helped him?" "How do you think your sister felt when you helped her with her homework?" "How do you think the boy felt when you shoved him into the locker?" "Why do you think the other boy didn't tell anyone you pushed him against the locker?" "What do you think he would tell you if he could?" "Why do you think your brother didn't want to share his toy with you?" "Why do you think I am upset by that phone call from the school?"

The next step is to help him recognize his own feelings and thoughts and take on the other person's perspective *before* he acts. "What did you feel before you shoved him into his locker?" "The next time you have those feelings, what can you do with them that will eliminate the possibility of your classmate being hurt by your actions? What can you do with those feelings that is more constructive?" "What did you feel before you twisted your brother's arm?" "What can you do the next time you feel that way?" "What was it that you felt you needed?" "How can you get what you need without hurting someone else?" "Can you imagine what the other child would think and feel if you called him such ugly names?" "Is there another way you could tell him what is bothering you?" "Would you want that said to you if you were in his shoes?" "What else could you do with your thoughts and feelings that would acknowledge your own wishes and still respect the dignity and worth of the other child?"

4. Teach friendship skills—assertive, respectful, and peaceful ways to relate to others.

There may be many reasons your son bullied his peer. It's okay to look for *explanations* as long as they are not seen as *excuses*. He may not have known how to be assertive or respectful, aggressively throwing his weight around and grabbing whatever it was that he wanted. He may not have known how to peacefully resolve inevitable peer conflicts. As he reacted aggressively to his peers, they began to see him as someone to fear and to stay away from or to "hang" with so as to avoid becoming one of his targets. Getting into the habit of acting tough and mean, he found himself with an inflated ego, not a strong sense of self; with acquaintances, not friends. Your child may have resorted to bullying because he couldn't figure out another way to make friends in a new situation. Anything he tried made matters worse, not better. He might have figured, "If I can't be the best, I'll be the worst."

To have friends, he needs to be a friend. In fact, one of the strongest buffers a child can have against being a bully is being a good friend. It is impossible to be a good friend and a bully at the same time. Being a friend is about caring and sharing. To learn how to be a good friend, your child first needs to understand three basic principles of any healthy relationship:

a. You control only 50 percent of the relationship with your classmate; he controls the other 50 percent. You can't *make* him play with you; you can only *invite* him to play. The choice to play with you or not is his to make. He doesn't have to accept your invitation to play.

b. You can *influence* 100 percent of the relationship. *How* you ask him to play can make a big difference in how your classmate responds. Yelling, berating, pushing, or hitting him will greatly reduce the chances of his ever wanting to play with you. Asking, sharing, complimenting, and encouraging him will greatly increase the likelihood that he will want to join in your activity.

c. "No" is a complete sentence. If your classmate doesn't want to play, no matter how respectfully you asked, no matter how much you want him to play, you must honour his "No" and go find someone else to play with you.

Knowing that you control 50 percent of a relationship and the other person controls the other 50 percent, that your words and actions influence the whole relationship, that you both can choose to accept or reject each other's invitations, and that "No" is a complete sentence can serve all three characters—the bullied, the bully, and the bystander—who are trying to change roles and break the cycle of violence. A child who is annoying you is only *inviting* you to pounce back; you don't *have* to accept the invitation. His annoying you never justifies bullying him. A bully's taunting is only an invitation to feel bad or to react aggressively or passively; you can turn it down. The bunch of bullies can invite you to join in the bullying of another child; you can say no and can invite the targeted child to join you in a more productive and creative endeavour. You could even invite the bully to join you (more on that later).

One of the hardest things for young people to grasp is the complexity of their social scene. In the insightful and humorous book *Cliques, Phonies, & Other Baloney*, Trevor Romain reminds kids that they always have a choice about their friendships. All kids want to feel they belong. But they don't need to be in a clique and, in fact, may not want to be in a clique. They can decide that being popular with their friends is the only popularity that really matters. "It's up to you. If you have one or two good friends, that's great. But you don't have to stop there. Use your people skills to make a few more friends. After all, you can never have too many people who care about you and like you for who you are." He goes on to give kids ways to be a good friend and thus keep friends:

The Top Ten Ways to Keep Your Friends

1. Show them kindness and respect.
2. Stick up for them.
3. Be supportive when your friends need help or advice.
4. Tell the truth (but be kind about it).
5. If you hurt a friend, say you're sorry.
6. If a friend hurts you and apologizes, accept the apology.
7. If you make a promise, keep it.
8. Put some effort into your friendships; otherwise your friends might feel neglected.
9. Don't try to change your friends—accept them the way they are.
10. Treat your friends the way you want them to treat you.
    And one more thing: Always be thankful for your friends.

A bully tries to boss or scare kids into doing what he wants them to do. ("If you want to play with me, you can't play with her.") A kid who wants to be a friend invites others to share in a relationship and then honours their acceptance or rejection of the invitation. Once someone accepts the invitation, a friend is careful to be assertive, respectful, and peaceful in his behaviour in order to keep her as a friend.

5. Closely monitor your child's TV viewing, video game playing, computer activities, and music.

In 374 BC, Plato wrote of his concern about negative influences on children's socialization: "And shall we just carelessly allow children to hear . . . tales which may be devised by casual persons, and to receive into their minds ideas for the most part the very opposite of those which we should wish them to have when they are grown up?" All forms of media have a profound effect on the way our children perceive the world in which they live. Media technology has become so powerful that we cannot afford to be laissez-faire about its consequences on our kids. Too much media involvement and too little "real-life" social interaction and engagement stifle the development of social skills necessary to relate in a decent, caring, and responsible way. Much of what is called entertainment certainly doesn't teach the basics of civility. Cruel, raunchy, crude, violent images and lyrics prevent the nurturing of empathy and respect, two critical elements of that civility. Teachers have reported an increase in "mob mentality" among kids who routinely watch "trash TV". Hoping to provoke a peer to lash out, students gang up and taunt her unmercifully with vile comments about her looks, behaviour, sexuality, or intellectual ability. So much for a thirty-minute character education lesson on the virtues of compassion, empathy, or respectful language. The television is a far more persuasive instructor than any class lecture on the importance of such virtues.

Research has shown that children who are regularly exposed to media violence are apt to become *desensitized* to real-life violence. As a consequence, they are less likely to be sensitive to the pain and suffering of others and thus less likely to respond to someone in need or to help out in a crisis. They are more likely to be *numb, apathetic, and callous* when they become aware of or see a peer being harmed. They are more willing to tolerate ever increasing levels of violence in their everyday world. They become habituated to a violent, crude, and rude society, taking it for granted and unable to visualize a life that is different.

The video game culture of violent fantasy seduces many emotionally vulnerable kids. When they are saturated with vivid media images glorifying violence as the legitimate solution to problems, they fail to learn peaceful conflict resolution skills. When they repeatedly play point-and-shoot video games that portray other people as adversaries, as prey, or as targets, they become desensitized to the act of shooting human beings, and the natural inhibition to killing people is broken down.

In the media, perpetrators of violence are almost always men. Young boys' impulses are being reinforced to commit acts of rape, murder, and sadism. Rapist and sadistic "entertainment" encourages denigration and subjugation of girls and women—talk about teaching contempt! Violence combined with sex is seen as fun, as sport. Add to the violence racist stereotyping, extreme competitiveness, greed, selfishness, and callousness and you have an instruction manual for bullying. In the media, people are often divided into "bad" people and "good" people—them and us. It is almost impossible to develop the ability to walk in another's shoes, respond compassionately, or see someone as an equal when they are "not one of us".

Kids *imitate* the violence they see and hear. There is a clear correlation between exposure to violence and the development and display of aggressive values and behaviour. Kids who habitually watch media violence tend to behave more aggressively and use aggression to try to solve problems. There is no correlation between what happens in real-life violence and the unreal media violence. In the media there are often no negative consequences for the perpetrators. If the perpetrator is viewed as a "good guy", violence is actually cheered and rewarded. Rarely is remorse shown, and even more rarely does a violent programme send any kind of antiviolence message.

Just as there are good movies and television shows, there are some fun games and fantasy games like MYST, one of the highest-selling games in the industry, which invite kids into a world that requires them to solve a mystery or accomplish a goal. There are many others that require little more than quick, aggressive, violent responses to a perceived threat. These games reward kids for their speed in reacting and for their quick reflexes. The reactive portions of their brains are strengthened. The abilities to reflect and respond are not reinforced; in fact, they are stifled. What is often reinforced are stereotypes, which in turn invite discrimination that can result in real-life discrimination. In his article "Culture Quake" (*Mother Jones*, November/December 1999), Paul Keegan describes the game QUAKE III: "[It] gives you only a few seconds to enjoy the medium before you get the message, loud and clear. As you drop hundreds of feet through space, you notice other inhabitants milling about on the landing platform below. Being a friendly sort, you approach them. Big mistake: They open fire. Reflexively, fearfully, you begin to shoot back. Heads and arms start exploding. In this magical environment, only one form of social exchange is permitted—kill or be killed. The images this astonishing new technology is most often called upon to render so lovingly are rivers of blood and chunks of torn flesh." *Reflexively* and *fearfully*—note that there is no time for reflection. Playing enough games like this over and over again, kids will be less tempted to assume the best of strangers they meet. It will be "smarter" to assume hostile intent in the behaviour of their classmates who are not in their own circle of caring.

A popular game with teen boys, GRAND THEFT AUTO, invites kids to kill police, blow up their cars with a bazooka, then machine-gun others and hear them scream. In this virtual reality, kids can go on to pick up a pair of prostitutes, spend time with them in a car, and then kick and beat them to the sidewalk—all these actions earning the player extra points. Such are the tales Plato wrote about "which may be devised by casual persons, and to receive into [our children's] minds ideas for the most part the very opposite of those which we should wish them to have when they are grown up."

Kids who are regularly exposed to media violence are apt to become *intimidated.* Believing the world is an unsafe and violent place, they become fearful and distrusting of others, overreacting to slights and minor incidents. The intimidation they feel can lead to depression—yes, bullies as well as their targets can become seriously depressed.

If your child is bullying others, chances are he will be more vulnerable to the effects of media violence. In an extensive quantitative review of the literature concerning television, researchers George Comstock and Haejung Paik concluded, "The strongest association between exposure to television violence and antisocial and aggressive behaviour is the amount of exposure both to television violence and to aggressive and antisocial behaviour." This conclusion has implications for both the bully and a child who is relentlessly bullied and has retreated to media violence as an escape from negative peer interactions.

What can you do as a parent?

a. Be aware of television shows, movies, DVDs, music, and computer games your children are exposed to on a daily basis. Become knowledgeable about them. Offer to watch, listen, and play them with your children so you know what ideas are "received into their minds".

b. Keep the television, DVD player, and computer in a family area.

c. Limit the amount of time for media exposure.

d. Teach critical thinking skills to assess the various media messages, intentions, and manipulative tools.

e. Expose your children to television shows, movies, plays, books, and games that teach values and virtues you would like them to learn.

f. Be alert to the four danger signs of overexposure to "uncivilizing" media: desensitization to violence, numbing, imitation, and intimidation.

g. Encourage kids to get involved with their peers in activities that promote creative, responsible, prosocial, and civil behaviours.

6. Engage in more constructive, entertaining, and energizing activities.

Your child can attack a rock-climbing wall with the same fervour he once used to attack his brother. This time, he will achieve a goal without "taking anyone out" in the process; he will feel a sense of accomplishment; and he can "do good" by teaching his brother to climb the same wall. He can "cruise" the river looking for great rapids to conquer rather than "cruise" the school hallways looking for weaker kids to bully out of their lunch money. He can throw a basketball through a hoop with the same energy and accuracy he had used to throw a punch at a peer. The more constructive, entertaining, and energizing activities your child engages in, the less time he will have to bully anyone else; the less he will need to use antisocial acts to get his needs met; the less likely he will be to even want to be antisocial. His poor social skills will be replaced with prosocial habits that reaffirm his own worth and abilities. He will be ready to take the next step in assuming a new role in his relationship with his peers—willing good.

7. Teach your child to "will good".

The real test of your child's ability to throw off the old role of bully and assume a new role of decent, caring, responsible human being will be when he is faced with a bully or a bunch of bullies who are taunting a peer. In his book *Integrity*, Stephen L. Carter writes of teaching children the concept of "willing good"—that is, speaking and doing what is right, "even when the burden is heavy". It involves helping children develop an inner moral voice (personal code) that guides them to do or say what is right, often in spite of external consequences and never merely because of them. This inner voice gives kids the strength to act with integrity when confronted with difficult situations, such as peer pressure intended to cause harm. Willing good involves three steps:

1. *Discerning what is right and what is wrong.* We can teach children the difference between right and wrong, but if they behave merely because they've been told to do so, or because they fear punishment, feel obligated, or are dependent on external approval, what we are trying to teach them will never become their personal code. If it never becomes their personal code, their conscience will

be available for sale to the highest bidder. ("I was only doing what I was told to do." "She made me do it." "She deserved to be teased." "Everyone else was doing it." "They told me I could join the group if I taunted him.") By being good and doing good, your child has begun to develop his own inner moral voice (personal code). He can begin to engage in self-talk about what his ideals are, what he stands for, and the kind of person he is trying to be. He has practised taking on another's perspective and feeling empathy toward that person. He will need courage to move to the next step.

2. *Act on what is right, even at personal cost.* "Hey, guys, back off, leave him alone." At this point, your child is choosing doing good over looking good to his friends. He is willing to take the sneers and jeers of his peers. ("Are you chicken?" "What, are you just like him?" "Look at Mister Goody Two-shoes over here.") Willing good involves both taking a stand and taking action. It is not enough for your child to feel the other child's pain. He must be willing to do something to alleviate it, even at the expense of alienating his friends. In his book *Can We Be Good Without God?* Dr Robert Buckman asks the question "Why should I behave decently?" His answer: "Because it will be a better world for the human race if we all do."

3. *Say openly that you are acting on your understanding of right and wrong.* "I'm not going to be a party to any of this, and I'll do whatever it takes to get this taunting to stop."

When your son chooses to will good, "even when the burden is heavy", he is reminding his peers that he is not ashamed of doing what he has discerned is right, even at great cost to himself. Your son has come full circle—from bullying another child to being a witness for that child. He will find with practice that this new role suits him fine and serves him well.

Know Thyself

Teaching your children to become assertive, not aggressive, to get their needs met in responsible, constructive ways, and to "be good", "do good", and "will good" takes time and effort on your part. It involves all of the steps above as well as taking stock of the way you get your own needs met, the way you handle minor and major conflicts in your own life, and the way you respond to your children's mistakes, mischief, and mayhem. But the time and effort are well worth it. There will be no more bullies in the house.

> *Children learn to care by experiencing good care. They come to know the blessings of gentleness, of sympathy, of patience and kindness, of support and backing, first through the way in which they themselves are treated.*

> —James L. Hymes Jr,
> *Teaching the Child Under Six*

CHAPTER SEVEN

Is There a Bullied Kid in the House?

The fundamental law of human beings is interdependence. A person is a person through other persons.

—Archbishop Desmond Tutu

As horrible as it is to find out that your child is bullying someone else, it is heartbreaking to suspect that your son or daughter is being bullied. As I mentioned in Chapter Three, don't count on your child telling you outright. Your daughter has good reasons for not walking in the door and declaring that her life is being made miserable by the bullies who refused to let her sit at their table in the lunchroom, pushed her off the swing, wrote ugly things about her on the toilet mirror, and taunted her as she waited for the bus. Your son has just as many good reasons for remaining quiet about being shoved into his locker, forced to hand over his jacket, called names in the hallway, tripped in PE class, and threatened with bodily harm if he didn't give up his lunch money. If you find out via the grapevine or through the telltale clues your kids are leaving, before you even think of confronting them with "Why didn't you tell me?" reflect on the reasons they may have kept the information from you:

- They are ashamed of being bullied.
- They are afraid of retaliation if they tell an adult.
- They don't think anyone *can* help them. They feel helpless.
- They don't think anyone *will* help them. They feel hopeless.
- They have bought into the lie that bullying is a necessary part of growing up.
- They may believe that adults are part of the lie—they bully the child, too, and minimalize the bullying.
- They have learned that "ratting" on a peer is bad, not cool, and "juvenile".

As I mentioned earlier, a deadly combination is a bully who gets what he wants from his target, a target who is afraid to tell, bystanders who either watch, participate, or look away, and adults who see bullying as teasing, as a necessary part of growing up, as "boys will be boys". Add to this combination the helplessness and hopelessness felt by the bullied child and the injunctions about "ratting", and there is a good chance that as a parent you could well be kept in the dark about the pain your children are experiencing every day at the hands of their peers or even at the hands of adults you have entrusted with your children.

The Clues Revisited

If your children know that they can come to you with the good, the bad, and the ugly, and that you will actively listen and offer your support, guidance, and wisdom, there is a chance they might tell you they are being bullied. Even if they don't come right out and tell you, if you take the time to have a dialogue with them about their everyday activities and if you are involved in their lives and know their friends, you are more apt to be tuned in to the clues that something is wrong. When you see these warning signs or clues that your child is being bullied, listen beyond the words and look beyond the actions:

1. Shows an abrupt lack of interest in school or a refusal to go to school.
2. Takes an unusual route to school.
3. Suffers a drop in grades.
4. Withdraws from family and school activities, wanting to be left alone.
5. Is hungry after school, saying he lost his lunch money or wasn't hungry at school.
6. Is taking parents' money and making lame excuses for where it went.
7. Makes a beeline for the toilet when she gets home.
8. Is sad, sullen, angry, or scared after receiving a phone call or an e-mail.
9. Does something out of character.
10. Uses derogatory or demeaning language when talking about peers.
11. Stops talking about peers and everyday activities.

12. Has dishevelled, torn, or missing clothing.
13. Has physical injuries not consistent with explanation.
14. Has stomachaches, headaches, panic attacks, is unable to sleep, sleeps too much, is exhausted.

As well as dialoguing with your children about everyday events and looking for warning signs, you can ask outright:

- Are there any bullies in your class?
- What kinds of things do they do or say?
- Are there any kids these bullies tend to pick on?
- Do they ever bully you?

No matter how you learn of the bullying, your first step is to respond to your child's expressed fears or signs of being bullied with encouragement, support, and love. She needs to know that nothing is too silly or too serious to talk about and that you are there as a caring adult to support and empower her.

A Few Do's and Don'ts

If you teach your kids to like themselves, to think for themselves, and to approach difficulties as problems to be solved, they are more likely to ask for your help, knowing from past experience that your help will be instructive and constructive—and not make the situation worse. They will also know that they can count on the following messages from you:

1. **I hear you; I am here for you; I believe you; you are not alone in this.** No matter what your child has to say or how

he is saying it, a good line for you is "Tell me about it", then be quiet and listen. Asking your child to talk about the bullying without your asking a lot of questions up front to frame his answers will give you insight into your child's perceptions, concerns, and anxieties. You may be able to get at reasons why the attack might have cut at the core of your child's sense of dignity and self-worth. (Is your child beating himself up for being beaten up by a bully? Is he ashamed of the way he responded or didn't respond to the bully? Was he humiliated by the peers who supported the bully and abandoned or shunned him?)

After your child has talked about his own hurt and pain, you can begin to gather the facts of who, where, and when. To jump immediately to the facts is to miss the most important part of the incident—what it has done to your child's sense of well-being.

2. **It is not your fault**. The blame belongs to the bully. No one deserves to be bullied. There may be behaviours that your child is engaging in that aggravate or annoy the bully (more on that later). But those behaviours never justify the contemptuous behaviour of the bully. This is no time for "If you would have . . . ", "If you didn't . . . ", "If you weren't so . . ." Remember, the bully has already demeaned your child: "You are not worthy of respect; you can't protect yourself; you have no control over what happens to you at school; and nobody likes you." Your child needs your help to counteract these ugly injunctions.

3. **There are things you can do.** "How can I help? You are not helpless and hopeless. And you don't need to do it alone. Together we can come up with an effective plan." You can

help your child figure out ways to assertively stand up to the bullying, steer clear of dangerous situations, take her power back, and more fully develop the gifts and skills she has. She will need your help to explore options, analyse choices, and eliminate those that would make the situation worse or would put her in more danger or provoke more violence. "How will that be helpful?" "What else can you do?" Once those are eliminated, she can act assertively on a constructive option.

4. **Report the bullying to school personnel.** Your child's teachers need to know about the bullying your child is experiencing. They need the facts—the date, time, place, kids involved, and specifics of the incidents—and the impact the bullying has had on your child. Follow up on the follow-through to make sure the adults are actively involved in protecting your child and any other child who is being bullied, and that the bully is not being punished or rescued but is in fact being disciplined. Older kids will not want you to be the one to approach the school—they fear your involvement will only make matters worse. And know that it could if the school community is not committed to dealing with bullying as the serious problem that it really is. (More on this in Chapter Nine, "Caring Schools, Involved Communities".)

There are five things you don't want to do:

1. **Don't minimize, rationalize, or explain away the bully's behaviour.** Bullying hurts a lot. No, the bully wasn't just teasing or flirting or having a conflict; and yes, the bully

144

intended harm. By minimizing, rationalizing, or trying to explain away the behaviour of the bully, you are inadvertently telling your child that she really is in this all alone. It won't take her long to figure out it's best to suffer in silence.

2. **Don't rush in to solve the problem for your child.** Unless your child is in serious physical danger, your *taking over* the situation will convey to your child that he is even more helpless than he thought, convey to the bully that your kid really is a vulnerable target, and convey to his peers that the bully had it right—your son is a "wimp" or, worse, a "mummy's boy". That said, we can't put all the responsibility on children to stop the bullying. We can give them tools to fend off and to stand up to a bully, but it is also our job as adults to create an environment that is not conducive to bullying and to confront bullying when we see it or hear about it. This is not the same as rushing in to take care of the bullying situation and rendering even more powerless the target. A bully learned to bully. She needs to learn how not to bully, and part of that teaching needs to be done by an adult. Since the majority of bystanders in some way support the bully, it is a *system* that has to be changed. All of the children playing out their own scripts are going to need support, instruction, and guidance to change the theme of their play.

3. **Don't tell your child to avoid the bully.** You are inadvertently telling him to keep running and hiding, remaining in fear of the bully. Bullies can "smell" that fear. Your son will begin to act like an ever-weakening victim and in turn signal to any and all bullies in the school yard

that he is an available target. It is okay to avoid the bully to avoid immediate and present danger, but it is not a long-term solution to the bullying. A sixteen-year-old complained to the principal of his high school that a group of kids were taunting him with ugly religious slurs and slamming him into lockers as he tried to get to class. The principal suggested he walk down another hallway, not just today until the problem could be addressed, but for the rest of the term. It is lousy when the onus is put on the target, not on the bullies.

4. **Don't tell your child to fight back.** Do you really want to teach your child that fighting is the answer? It isn't, and besides, the bully probably picked on your son because he saw him as a less than equal match. After your child loses, there will be bigger bullies waiting for him. Defend himself, yes. Be assertive, yes. But being assertive more often than not will involve your child using his head and his feet—in that order. "This is a dumb place to be; I'm out of here." He heads out not because he is chicken, but because he is smart. Kids who respond assertively to the bully are more likely to successfully counteract the bullying than kids who try to fight back.

5. **Don't confront the bully or the bully's parents alone.** The bully learned to bully somewhere, and it might just be from his parents. They may be defensive and uncooperative and quick to blame the target. When the mother of a bully was confronted with the fact that her seven-year-old daughter had enlisted the help of several classmates to circle another classmate and call the targeted girl "brown and ugly", the mother insisted that her

daughter wouldn't do such a thing, and that even if she did, the other little girl must have asked for it.

If at all possible, enlist the help of a school counsellor to confer with you and your child and then with the bully and the bully's parents. (More on this in Chapter Nine, "Caring Schools, Involved Communities.")

Telling and Tattling—Discerning the Difference

Children need to know that they can and should tell an adult about the bullying, *even if they were able to stop the bullying themselves.* If not confronted, the bully will find another child to harass—one who may not be as capable of fending off the bully. A target who tells an adult in order to prevent someone else from sharing the same fate is playing the all-important role of witness.

As I noted, most bullying is done "under the radar" of adults, and children are hesitant to report it. We have to convince our children that we can be trusted, are powerful allies, and will act— if only they would tell us. That requires that we teach them to discern the difference between telling and tattling.

From the time our children begin telling tales on their siblings and peers, we admonish them, "Don't tattle, don't snitch." Then, when kids keep potentially lethal information from us, we ask, "Why didn't you tell me?" Even the words we use—tattle, snitch, rat, squeal, fink—have a harshness that communicates to our kids that it's not a good thing to ever tell on anybody. These words entrench children in the deeply embedded code of silence. What is lost in this code is the immorality of that silence in the face of malice.

Just as we can teach our kids the difference between teasing and taunting, flirting and harassing, and fighting and bullying, we can teach them the difference between telling and tattling. I use a simple formula:

- Tattling: If it will only get another child *in* trouble, don't tell me.
- Telling: If it will get you or another child *out* of trouble, tell me.
- If it is *both*, I need to know.

This formula does not tell kids what to report to an adult. It is a tool to help them *discern* what to tell, no matter what kind of situation they are facing.

Using everyday events as opportunities to practise, you can start teaching four-year-olds the difference between telling and tattling. "James is sucking his thumb again." (Telling me is an attempt to get him in trouble; don't tell.) "James's front tooth fell out, and his mouth is all bloody." (Telling me can get him out of a mess; tell.) "James's front tooth fell out when he was sucking his thumb, and his mouth is a bloody mess." (It's both; I need to know.) By the time kids are six, they can be taught the difference between teasing and taunting and sibling rivalry and bullying. If Johnny isn't sharing the swing, telling me will only get him in trouble, so don't tell me. Use your skills that I've taught you to negotiate with him. Remember, he controls 50 percent of the relationship—and at this point 100 percent of the swing. You control 50 percent of the relationship; you both can influence 100 percent of the relationship; and "No" is a complete sentence. If Johnny knocked Jeff off the swing and called him an ugly name, tell me, I need to know. If Susie is telling all the girls in sixth grade to exclude the new girl to see if she has what it takes to survive three weeks of being shunned, tell me, I need to know.

If this distinction is taught to children when they are young, it can pay off in the teen years. Adolescents will understand that it is not tattling, snitching, ratting, or squealing to tell you that their friend who has been tormented by peers is giving his possessions away and saying subtle goodbyes to classmates. Telling may help get him out of the mess he is in; not telling could be life-threatening. Your daughter's girlfriend who is five months' pregnant and is binding herself up in an attempt to hide her pregnancy has sworn your daughter to secrecy about the baby. Telling might get her in trouble with some people, but it will certainly get her and her baby out of trouble. Your daughter has the tools to discern what to do. Will she do it? We don't know, but having the tools will help. There is going to be a fight after school, and an arsenal of weapons has been hidden in the lockers of rival teens; telling will get kids in trouble in the short term but out of big trouble and serious regret in the long term.

Julie's telling her mum about Meridith challenging Meghan to pull her trousers down in the playground or risk being permanently ostracized from the group (Chapter Two) was a matter of getting someone in trouble and someone out of trouble. Julie knew she could talk to her mum and that her mum would believe her and do something about the situation. In the end, all three girls benefited from her telling.

As well as practising with everyday situations, keep the lines of communication open by being truly present and listening to what your kids are saying—or trying to say—with their fumbled words, body language, and actions. Kids won't say a word if they think their telling will be met with judgmental statements, disbelief, or threats: "Don't say such crazy things." "Don't tattle." "He wouldn't kill himself." "If I ever catch you doing something as stupid as he did, you'll be grounded." What teen would want to hear that his friend wouldn't be stupid enough to kill himself, that her pregnant friend is a slut, that fights like that don't happen in this part of town? Imagine what might have happened if Julie's mum had insisted that nobody would make a girl do that in the playground, or said that Julie must be mistaken or that it was not her problem?

That is what happened to Andy Williams's friends. On March 4, 2001, in Santee, California, fifteen-year-old Andy Williams boasted at a weekend sleepover of his plan to kill kids at his school. An adult, overhearing the plan, told the boy that if he ever said things like that again, the adult would turn him in to the police. To that threat, Andy responded, "I was just kidding." The next day, Andy killed two kids and wounded thirteen more at his school. He wasn't kidding; he was trying to speak of unspeakable torment and hurt that had turned to rage.

Some of Andy's friends had been concerned enough to tell their own parents about the threat. One parent laments the fact she dismissed her own son's concern with the comment, "Don't be silly, he wouldn't do such a thing." These same friends were concerned enough to pat Andy down when he arrived at school that day, but they missed the loaded handgun in his backpack. "We didn't think he was serious." "If we'd told, it would have gotten him in trouble." "He was teased a lot, picked on every day."

One can only wonder what would have happened had an adult been aware of Andrew's pain, taken the boy aside, and offered a "Talk to me about it", alerted the boy's parent, asked the parent about the child's access to a weapon, and notified someone at the school of the rage this boy was expressing; if his friends had reported the plan to adults who had taken them seriously; if taunting a boy were not considered an okay thing to do; if . . .

That same week, an eight-year-old girl reported that a classmate had threatened to kill her. She was listened to and taken seriously; the loaded gun was confiscated from the eight-year-old boy's backpack. Yes, the boy is in serious trouble, but a lot less trouble than he'd be in if he had shot the girl. And the girl is alive to tell how she learned when to tell and whom to tell.

Four Antidotes to Bullying

The four most powerful antidotes to bullying are a strong sense of self, being a friend, having at least one good friend who is there for you through thick and thin, and being able to successfully get into a group. A bully will try to sabotage all of these, first by harassing your child, chipping away at his sense of dignity and worth; second by effectively isolating him so that he is unable to develop critical relationship skills with his peers; and third by enlisting peers to join in or at least not stop the bullying—further shutting your child off from any positive peer relationships and critical friendships. Being bullied can lead to further rejection by peers. At a time when he is most in need of support from them, he is least likely to receive it. It seems nobody likes him no matter how hard he tries to fit in and be accepted. Your child begins to see school as a threatening, lonely place where he can't count on anyone to help him out. The more he is bullied without any relief or intervention, the more he will have to change what he does, where he goes, and whom he can hope to socialize with. The cycle of violence grinds on.

The cycle of violence is easier to break early on; but no matter when in the cycle you become aware of your child being bullied, you can help him strengthen his sense of self, show him how to be a good friend, teach him how to nurture strong, healthy friendships, and teach him how to introduce himself into a group. In a 1990 thesis, "The Behavioral Attributes of Victimized Children", doctoral student S. Pierce wrote about the five personality factors that seemed to protect kids from becoming increasingly victimized over the course of the school year: 1. friendliness, 2. willingness to share, 3. willingness to cooperate, 4. skill in joining the play of other children, and 5. possessing a sense of humour—all factors critical to the four antidotes to bullying.

Strong Sense of Self

If your kids see themselves as being capable, competent, cooperative, responsible, resourceful, and resilient, not only are they less likely to be cruel and combative bullies, they are more likely to be able to effectively fend off an attack by one. As you saw in "Scenes from a Tragedy" in Chapter One, the first response of a bullied child is critical. When a bully comes along who has contempt for a particular group and your children fit in that group, they may get targeted no matter how tall they stand, how secure they look, how quick with words they are. To tell kids that if they use their bully-proofing skills, a bully won't target them is a lie—a hopeful one, but a lie nevertheless. The reality is that the better your children feel about themselves, the less likely they are to *succumb* to the tactics of a bully should one be so foolish as to target them.

Children who use positive self-talk to develop confidence and respect for themselves are more likely to see the cause of the bullying as coming from the *outside* and, therefore, not something to beat themselves up over. The line I like to give children is, "I am a decent, caring, responsible person. I didn't ask for this. I don't deserve this. That bully made a mistake, is obviously having a lousy day, and is trying to get his needs met in a mean way." Sometimes these lines are best spoken under their breath as they walk away from the taunting; sometimes the words are spoken directly to the bully. Either way, the bullied child affirms his own dignity and self-worth and begins to put the problem where it belongs—with the bully.

On the other hand, if your child lacks a strong sense of self, is praise-dependent, and tends to beat herself up for things that go wrong in her life, she will likely blame herself for being bullied. Kids who blame themselves for being bullied are more likely to succumb to the tactics of a bully and become vulnerable to more attacks. If they think the attacks are directed at something inherent in their makeup or character, they are more likely to get depressed and anxious (I am stupid, I am ugly, I am clumsy, I am friendless, I am inferior, I am crazy). When they ask the question "Why me?" they are right there bullying themselves to validate why the bully targeted them. These thoughts are self-defeating and reinforce their feelings of helplessness and hopelessness.

When kids practise the art of self-affirmation—positive self-talk—they tend to feel better about themselves. You can't just teach kids to mouth the self-affirming lines. Kids need people in their lives who offer them encouragement, feedback, and unconditional love. And they have to be guided to behave in ways that make them feel and act like decent, caring, and responsible people who like themselves, think for themselves, and know they are capable of solving problems. If you look at the traits of the caring family (Chapter Five), you will see it is the backbone family that provides the structure for kids to flesh out the strong sense of self needed to rebuff the bully. Kids in a backbone family can freely express their feelings, make mistakes, grow from those mistakes, and know that they can act in their own best interests, stand up for themselves, and exercise their rights while respecting the rights and legitimate needs of others.

Sometimes self-affirmation is not enough. Your kids will need comeback lines—assertive retorts to the bullying. It is important that these one-liners be assertive, not aggressive or passive.

Aggression—be it verbal, physical, or relational—only begets more aggression. Kids who respond aggressively to an attack, angrily striking at the bully, usually end up losing the struggle. The bully was no fool and now has a target who is distressed, frustrated, and defeated.

In my research for this book, I came across some disturbing aggressive one-liners a psychologist recommended targets say to the bully. I think these would probably agitate a bully even more and make a first-class bully out of your child as well.

These are lines I suggest you *not* give your child:

- Respond with a comment like "It takes one to know one".
- Reverse the teasing. Give the bully the same put-down.
- Call the bully by name and ask, "What did you say?" and "Could you say that again?" The bully may repeat what he or she said two or three times. Then you, in a condescending manner, say something like "Good boy, Sam! You said that three times."

- Make the bully look foolish when he or she says something obvious. Example: "He noticed that I don't have any hair. Wow!"
- Make fun of the bully for repeating taunts: "You keep saying the same thing over and over. Can you say it in a different way, or even sing it?"

Why would anyone recommend that you teach your child to ridicule, taunt, make condescending comments, or make fun of another person—even if that person is a bully? We can begin to break the cycle of violence by confronting that kind of speech when we hear it and eliminating it from our own vocabulary. As my twenty-four-year-old son would say, "Don't even put it out in the universe." There is a Buddhist aphorism that states: "Believe nothing merely because you have been told it. . . . But whatsoever, after due examination and analysis, you find to be kind, conducive to the good, the benefit, the welfare of all beings—that doctrine believe and cling to and take as your guide." None of those one-liners is kind, conducive to the good, or to the benefit and welfare of anybody.

Passivity, however, invites further aggression. Kids who respond passively to an attack—slumping over, begging, pleading, or quickly submitting to a bully's demands—only encourage the bully to keep up the bullying. Lines that a child might say to a friend who has inadvertently hurt him can backfire when said to a bully. "Hey, that hurts." "Don't do that. I don't like it." "Please leave me alone, I don't like what you're doing." To the ears of a bully, they are invitations to keep bullying. To cry in front of a bully or to let him know you don't like what he is doing is letting him know he has accomplished his goal. He'll crank up the volume and intensity of his contemptuous behaviour. And each time he does so, his innate ability to feel any empathy is stifled, his sense of shame is diminished, his callousness grows thicker.

Assertive lines and actions have the potential to dissipate the aggression of the offending party, and they will most certainly leave intact the dignity and self-worth of the person speaking the lines. "Yikes! I'm not up for this. I'm out of here." "Wow, man, you poured that on thick; I don't need this; I'm gone." "That was a gross thing to do. It's beneath both of us." These lines can be spoken out loud or said as self-talk. Either way, they affirm the targeted child's power to control how he acts and what he does with what the bully is throwing at him. In her book, *Tongue Fu!*, Sam Horn explains why assertive lines have a chance at stopping a bully: "Bullies push, push, push as a way of taking your measure. They test people to see what they're made of. In a perverse way, they admire only the ones who say, 'You're not getting away with that here'."

THE GORMANS OF THE WORLD

Michael McMannis, a Canadian television producer, shared with me the story of his being bullied and the assertive one-liner his father gave him.

> Every day just before noon, Gorman, a big boy who sat directly behind me, placed his fist in my face and demanded, "You owe me!" I would run home for lunch and steal money out of my mother's purse to turn over to Gorman in the afternoon. After weeks of stealing money,

my guilty feelings overrode the fear I had of Gorman. I told my father what I had done and why I did it. My dad said, "Michael, you are going to run into Gormans all your life. You need to stand up to him and let him know it's over, the game's up, that you won't be intimidated by the likes of his kind."

I walked to school the next day practising what I would say to the bully. When the fist came, I turned around in my seat, sat tall, and spoke the words my dad had given me the night before: "It's over, Gorman. There will be no more money." At that point, Gorman looked much smaller to me and I felt much bigger and stronger. I never saw that fist in my face again.

Will standing tall, walking confidently and with purpose, and speaking assertively always do the trick? No, but it is one more valuable script your child will have. The key is to have several well-rehearsed scripts and a few actions readily available, with the ability to discern which one is the most appropriate for the given situation. Sometimes words spoken under your breath are best, sometimes words spoken out loud are, sometimes yelling for help is better, and there are times when you had best save your breath and start running. As Trevor Romain suggests in *Bullies Are a Pain in the Brain*, "You might look a bit foolish running down the street like a maniac, but you will look *alive*." And there are times when handing over money or a jacket is the wisest thing to do. Your children need to know that nothing they own is worth more than their safety.

A pre-emptive assertive action is to be friendly with a potential bully. In their 1998 study, S. K. Egan and D. G. Perry noted that children who are "agreeable" communicate to other children that they like them, and other children—even aggressive ones—are inclined to reciprocate the liking and thus avoid attacking them. I can attest to their findings from firsthand experience. In the summer of 1970, I was lifeguarding at a pool in north Denver. After weeks of failed negotiations with the powers-that-be in the Department of Parks and Recreation, in an attempt to get improvements to the swimming pool that would be equal to improvements at pools in the more affluent parts of Denver, a group of angry teens took matters into their own hands. They stormed the pool, wreaking havoc with the deteriorating diving boards, showers, and dressing rooms, as well as roughing up the guards. As four kids grabbed me, the leader of the "pool takeover" yelled at them to let me go. I quickly scrambled over the chain-link fence and ran home. Weeks later, after the pool had been repaired and upgraded, I ran into the young man whose command to his henchmen had spared me the roughing-up my fellow guards endured. I asked him why he had told the four to let me go. He shrugged and said, "Because you were kind to me once."

Three vital elements to a child responding assertively are a *belief* that no one can strip her of her own sense of dignity and worth, an *understanding* that she can control how she responds to a bully, and a *refusal* to get down in the mud with a bully and bully back.

Buddies, Friends, and Other Former Strangers

Stopping bullying is harder than preventing it in the first place. Having older kids as buddies, being a friend, and knowing how to hang around with potential friends can radically reduce bullying incidents your child might encounter.

BUDDIES

If your child is at risk of being bullied on the way to school, on the bus, in the playground, in the lunch room, or in the hallways, it is helpful to find an older child to be your child's buddy. And since any child could possibly be at risk, an ideal plan is to "buddy" kids up early in the school year. The buddy programme can serve a dual purpose: The younger child is less likely to be targeted by a peer when he has a bigger kid right next to him who is in a sense "protecting" him; and older kids who are buddies to younger children are less likely to bully any younger children. These older kids are too busy "being good", "doing good", and "willing good" to have the time or inclination to target someone smaller. The three essentials for successful peer relationships— empathy, compassion, and perspective-taking—are nurtured and strengthened. Some of the best buddies are reformed bullies. Their leadership skills and power that were inappropriately used to wreak havoc in the past can be great assets to them in their new role.

FRIENDS

Just as being a friend can be good for a bully who is trying to turn his life around, it is equally good for a child who could be a target for a bully. Friendship skills play an important role in preventing bullying, buffering kids from the harmful effects of bullying, and helping kids cope after a bullying episode.

Children need to be taught to make friends wisely, to keep friendships growing, and to walk away from friendships that are harmful. "The Ten Top Ways to Keep Your Friends" listed on page 129 work for bullied kids as well as for bullies. In his book, *Nurturing Good Children Now*, Dr Ron Taffel writes about what he sees as the single most important factor in the development of these basic friendship skills—the way children are treated at home. "If we are accepting or critical, inclusive or exclusive, demanding or giving, relaxed or anxious, if we encourage siblings to be loving or allow them to mistreat one another at home—all of these behaviours can affect the kinds of friends our children choose." The way we interact at home also influences the way our children develop their social skills that help them make and keep friends. Your children need the opportunity to develop their abilities to listen, exchange ideas, and work with others toward a common goal. They need to be able to control their own behaviour and anticipate the consequences of words they speak and actions they take. Kids bring to school the attitudes and behaviours they learned at home.

Kids who annoy or irritate their peers are at great risk not only of being the target of a bully, but of becoming increasingly isolated from even caring and compassionate peers. The more isolated they become, the higher their risk of being vulnerable targets, with bullies and bystanders joining forces against them. In turn, they are likely to become seriously depressed or enraged. If your child is unwittingly contributing to rejection by his peers, he will need your help to find a solution to his problem. Be aware of how he behaves in his social circle. He may be resorting to inappropriate social tactics either because he does not know better or because he has run out of appropriate options in his repertoire of friendship skills.

It is important that your child know how to accurately read social cues—words, actions, and body language. Kids help teach one another about social behaviours—what works and what doesn't; what is acceptable and what is not; what's funny and what is hurtful humour. Your child needs to notice how others are reacting to her behaviour and recognize the *cues* her peers are giving her that are *clues* to what is working and what is not. "Tell me what happened when you grabbed the toy." "Did everyone walk away when you started to act silly?" "Did your classmate frown when you commented on his outfit?" "Did everyone laugh at the joke?" "Did the target of the joke give any signals that he was hurt by what was said?" "What can you do when your behaviour is annoying someone?" "One of your friends is crying. What can you say and do?"

If your child has a serious handicap or learning disability, he has a risk factor for putting him on the radar screen of the bully, but he will be at far greater risk if he lacks necessary friendship skills. In fact, friendship skills can mitigate a handicap or disability. A word of caution is due here. As much as you have taught your child who has a disability to be kind, caring, and accepting, you must also teach him to be wary, sceptical, and willing to be rude if necessary to protect himself from unscrupulous peers who "buddy" up to him in order to glean enough information to be used against him. Jeremy, a boy with a lisp, was asked by a group of ten-year-old boys to read aloud the poem he had written. He happily read the poem, only to have one boy repeat it—lisp and all—as the other boys laughed. Your child needs real friends who can help him see when someone is trying to "use" him, clue him in, and stand by him.

The quality of your child's friendships matter. If your bullied daughter is hanging around exclusively with another child who has been bullied, the two of them are more likely to spend their time commiserating with each other and making each other feel even more miserable. Misery loves company. But neither girl will have the strength to support each other or stand up for each other. If your bullied son is hanging around with another bullied boy, the two of them are more likely to fuel each other's rage and spend time concocting ways to seek revenge on their nemesis and anyone else who failed to come to their aid. All four bullied kids need support and guidance to either turn these friendships into strong, helpful ones or to move beyond them into more positive friendships.

The former may actually be easier than the latter. Inviting either twosome to join you in challenging activities that require cooperation, strategizing, and supporting each other in order to accomplish a common goal can build both kids up and create a friendship devoid of the negative energies that brought the two together in the first place. Encouraging them to get involved in "doing good" in the community also enables them to get "outside" of themselves. It's hard to be miserable and giving at the same time.

OTHER FORMER STRANGERS

Just as being a friend and having friends are antidotes to bullying, so is a child's ability to introduce herself into a group. Kids who find themselves alone in the playground, unwilling or unable to join in a game or other social activity, are prime targets for bullies. If your daughter looks like a shrinking violet against the school wall or your son appears to be playing hide-and-seek, with him hiding and only bullies seeking him out, they both need to learn useful and effective ways to introduce themselves into a group and how to conduct themselves once they join—for example, observe, ask a question or say something positive about the group, ask to play or join, cooperate, play fair, share, and resolve conflicts nonviolently. You can help them role-play various situations where they ask to join and are welcomed, rejected, or ignored. How they handle all three of these situations will increase or decrease their chances of being a part of any group in school.

They also need to be able to evaluate the various groups and recognize that some groups are better to be a part of than others. Some groups help them learn to get along with others and help them develop close friendships with people who enjoy doing the same things they like to do. Some groups help them feel good by doing good deeds in the community. Some groups thrive on having a scapegoat and might welcome your daughter to play the part. Others find their pleasure by regularly excluding selected targets. Your empathic son may struggle with the conflicted feelings of belonging to a group and hurting someone in a way he knows only too well. If your child finds himself in a group that purposely excludes other kids, makes other kids feel unwelcome, is mean to kids in the group or to a select few outside of the group, or requires that he conform to standards with which he is uncomfortable or do things he doesn't really want to do, it's time for him to find a new group of real friends who care about themselves, one another, and others outside of their group. The question your child needs to ask himself to determine if the group is a good one to join is "Can I be good (and true to myself), do good, and will good in this group?"

Negotiation and Conflict Resolution Skills

Kids who spend a lot of time together are guaranteed to have squabbles and get into fights. It is important that your child learn to solve problems and resolve conflicts peacefully. Both of these require that your child be able to be understanding of a friend's wishes and needs and assertive about her own. They also involve the ability to reach cooperative solutions centred on kindness and fairness. The following is a summary of the essentials.

PROBLEM SOLVING

No matter what the problem, solving it usually involves these six steps:

1. Identify and define the problem.
2. List viable options for solving the problem.
3. Evaluate the options—explore the pros and cons for each option.
4. Choose one option.
5. Make a plan and do it.
6. Evaluate the problem and your solution: What brought it about? Could a similar problem be prevented in the future? How was the present problem solved?

When kids present their own ideas, listen to each other's reasoning, and work cooperatively to arrive at a solution, they learn that there is not always a definite right or wrong; there is no one correct way to solve most problems. The give-and-take, openness, and cooperation on the part of both children help them bond with each other. Kids who have solved problems successfully together are more likely to come to each other's aid when either is being bullied.

RESOLVING CONFLICTS PEACEFULLY

The same is true if these friends have been able to peacefully resolve the conflicts they will inevitably encounter. Example is a powerful way to teach. If we see conflict as a contest, we will probably fight physically or verbally with our "opponents" until one of us has won and one is soundly defeated. We can run from conflict, showing our children how to run as well. We can also model resolving conflict assertively, without aggression or passivity. We can teach our kids constructive alternatives to the instincts to fight, flee, or freeze. We can teach them through example, guidance, and instruction that violence is an immature, irresponsible, and unproductive technique for resolving conflict and that using nonviolent tools to resolve conflict is a mature and courageous act. This involves teaching kids to listen to all sides of the story, to use their heads before using their mouths, and to come up with a plan both kids can accept.

Sharing their feelings will help them learn to be less quick to judge and more able to be compassionate. Here's a simple format kids can learn:

When I heard (or saw) . . .	**not** When you said (or did) . . .
I felt . . .	**not** You made me angry.
because I . . .	**not** I couldn't help it.
I need (or want) . . .	**not** You'd better, or else.

It takes time to teach kids to handle their feelings assertively, but in doing so you teach them that their own feelings are important, that they can be trusted to handle those feelings, and that they can count on you for support and guidance when they have handled them poorly.

After both children have shared their feelings, they can move on to examining the five ingredients necessary for the peaceful resolution to the conflict:

1. Identify the issues that underlie the incident.
2. Figure out how each person contributed to causing the dispute.
3. Think about what you are willing to do to bring about a resolution.
4. Be prepared for both of you making concessions.
5. Ask yourselves, "What do we want to have come out of this?"

Then together they can come up with a solution both can accept. It will be a solution formed with a greater understanding of each other's wants, needs, feelings, and perceptions.

Children need to be assured and reminded that in attempting to resolve any conflict, it is okay to:

1. **call time out.** ("We are both too angry to talk right now. Let's talk about this later." "I'm too upset to work through this right now. I need to take a break.") If either child is too angry or too upset to speak calmly and responsibly, it is important to call time out and come back to the process later.
2. **refuse to take abuse.** ("It hurts when you say those things about me." "You can be angry at me, but you can't hit me.")

If one child becomes verbally, physically, or emotionally abusive, the other child has a right to refuse to take the abuse.

3. **insist on fair treatment.** ("I won't borrow your pen without asking you first, and I want you to ask me first if you can borrow mine." "It's not fair for you to always be the one to get the ball at breaktime just because you can run faster than the rest of us. We've got to come up with a better solution.") Fair treatment is not always equal or identical treatment, but it is *honest, adequate, and just.*

Through our own example, resolving family disputes, and playing out "what if" scenarios with our children about their social situations, we can help them learn to recognize when it is necessary to call time out and that they have the right to be treated with respect, dignity, and fairness. They also have the responsibility not to let their feelings take over the situation; to see that they do not physically, verbally, or emotionally abuse another person; and to treat other people with the same dignity they themselves hope for. Resolving conflicts peacefully enables kids to use their feelings as a positive energy source to establish and maintain productive relationships with each other.

We can impart to our children the wisdom of the peacemakers: Peace is not the absence of conflict. It is the embracing of conflict as a challenge and an opportunity to grow.

Unmasking Anger, Calming Rage

Holocaust survivor Elie Wiesel was asked about his memoir, *Night,* in which he wrote about the Hungarian soldiers who drove him and his family from their home. " 'It was from that moment that I began to hate them, and that hate is still the only link between us today,' " he responded. "I wrote that, but I didn't hate. I just felt terribly angry and humiliated . . . I was terribly disappointed. I used the word *hate* because that was the strongest feeling I could imagine having. But when I think about it now, there was no hate in me. I grew up learning that hate destroys the hater as much as its victims." (*O* magazine, November 2000.)

Anger, humiliation, and disappointment—if your child has been bullied, he is probably feeling all of these emotions. The way he may express them is by saying he *hates* the bully, all those who joined in, laughed, stood idly by, or turned away, and the adults who did nothing to stop the bullying. What Elie Wiesel understood was that the word *hate* was really concealing more fundamental responses to the horrific indignities and inhumane treatment he witnessed and endured during the war. When the word *hate* was stripped away, anger, humiliation, and disappointment were still there. They needed to be acknowledged and accepted if Elie Wiesel was to resist being consumed or crippled by them.

Your child will need to do the same with his feelings. But first your child needs to know it is all right to feel. Feelings are not good or bad per se. It's what your child does with his feelings that makes all the difference. Feelings are motivators for growth or warning signs that something needs to change. Trying to cover up the grief will not serve your child ("Come on, cheer up, just get over it; he won't hurt you again"). He needs to mourn any loss, be it loss of security, belongings, sense of well-being, academic progress, or social interactions. To make light of the incidents will only help the bullied child bury the pain deeper into himself—and it will stay there to fester. To shrug off his own feelings ("It wasn't much. It doesn't matter, really. I'll be okay. Let's drop it") is to dismiss the important messages his legitimate feelings are sending.

To tell a child he can't or shouldn't be angry is to deny him a way to heal from his hurt and the opportunity to move on from the bullying. It also locks your child into viewing himself as a helpless victim and the bully in the one-dimensional role as oppressor. Your child could spend his days vengefully scheming ways to punish the bully. To heal and move on, he must be able to tell his story and be believed, have his pain acknowledged and his anger expressed. After he is able to say, "I am angry," you can help him unmask the anger and calm his rage. Anger is unmasked by helping your child answer the following questions:

- Where did it come from? ("From inside myself. The bully did not make me angry.")
- Is it masking another feeling? ("I am hurt, scared the bully will hurt me again, humiliated by what happened to me, disappointed in how my peers acted, and disillusioned by the adults who wouldn't listen.")
- Can I feel all of those feelings and still have anger? ("Yes. Denying anger, stuffing it down, or striking out won't get rid of the anger.")
- Why be angry, anyway? ("Because I care. If I didn't care, I wouldn't be angry. I can't be angry about something I don't care about.")

In *Yoga and the Quest for the True Self*, psychotherapist and senior Kripalu yoga teacher Stephen Cope writes of anger "as an energy existing, like all emotions, halfway between physical and mental experience. Like heat or other energies, anger wanes naturally if we don't hold it back with psychological defences. . . . Anger tends to arise in a very visceral wave. It arises, crests, and then passes away." The five sequential steps for the techniques he calls "riding the wave" can help your child stay with the raw feeling of anger without acting on it "until you're really clear".

1. *Breathe deeply.* This breathing will help your child take his mind off the physical tension in his body, the incidents, and the feeling of anger.
2. *Relax.* As he relaxes his muscles, the energy of the anger is accepted, not fought or acted upon.
3. *Feel.* By focusing on what his body is feeling and where in the body he is feeling it, he can explore how he uniquely manifests anger. Does his stomach churn? Do his shoulders tense? Is he quick to react? Does he let it overwhelm him? Does his mind move quickly to revenge? Does he beat himself up with the anger?
4. *Watch.* If your child can observe the sensation he is feeling, he can "make discerning choices about how to respond to it rather than reacting to it".
5. *Allow.* Not resisting the anger, but accepting it and watching it go through the body, allows your child to calm down and clear his mind so that he can decide what he needs to do and what he needs from the bully.

Once your child is clear on what he needs from the bully, the two of them can come together. If your child can get the assurance of safety and adult and peer support during the time it takes him to move through the anger and honour his sadness, he will find himself ready to look for creative solutions to solving the problems that both he and the reformed bully face in order to be reconciled. As I mentioned in the last chapter, this is not the same as seeing bullying as a conflict. The problems that need to be solved relate to how the two can live together in the school community after the bullying has been stopped and after the bully has worked through the steps of discipline. The bullied child has the power of choice this time around.

Even if the reformed bully came to your son with a heartfelt apology and offer of restitution, your child might want more time to become stronger himself before he can reconcile. The *intention* behind asking for time is not to hurt the bully, to make him feel the same pain he inflicted, or to make him suffer as much as your child suffered. The time may be needed for your child to face the hurt, to identify and express his emotions, and to begin to release any grudges and destructive feelings, so that he not only reclaims his own peace of mind, his sense of security and safety and well-being, he can also begin to open his heart and his hands to reconciliation with the other boy. If they both use the time that leads up to the reconciliation constructively, the two children who come together for this step will not only interact differently from past encounters, they will be very different kids from the bully and the bullied kid who had been caught in the cycle of violence.

Self-Defence

I am asked often if putting a child in a self-defence class will help him or her strike back effectively against a bully. Striking back is the wrong goal. We want our children to be able to defend themselves. All three of my children studied aikido, a martial art that by its nature is *defensive*, not *offensive*. If a bully tries to strike, the target "moves" with the hit and harnesses the energy, ideally becoming a partner with the aggressor but in a way that dissipates the aggressive energy of the bully. ("That was a gross thing to do. It's beneath both of us.") Practising aikido (or any other defensive martial art) helps your children resist reacting out of fear, focus themselves, get in touch with their inner calm, and have clarity of mind. When involved in the study of such a martial art, your children will tend to present themselves physically in an assertive manner, standing tall, head up, confident in their stride and strong in their voice.

In their book, *Aikido and the Dynamic Sphere*, Adele Westbrook and Oscar Ratti write of the ethics of self-defence according to Master Uysehiba's method: "A man must sincerely desire to defend himself without hurting others." The authors explain four levels of interaction between two people. Translated into a bully and a bullied child's encounters, they involve the following:

1. A bully, without provocation and on his own initiative, attacks the target and harms him. This is the lowest of the four levels of ethical behaviour—unprovoked aggression in the form of an attack.
2. A bully tries to provoke the target to attack him through "obvious provocation, such as an insulting remark or more subtle provocation of a contemptuous attitude". When the target is invited to attack and does so, once again the target is harmed—physically, emotionally, or, as

was the case with Rangi from New Zealand, suspended from school for supposedly starting the fight that was actually provoked by the other boys in the classroom. There is only a "shade of difference ethically" between this level and the lowest one.

3. The target neither attacks nor provokes the bully to attack. But when attacked, "he defends himself in a subjective manner, i.e., he takes care of only 'number one'." Either the bully or the target is seriously harmed. Ethically this is a more defensible action than the other two. This is the tactic most commonly recommended by parents of boys—be tough, suppress emotions, and strike back. ("If he hits you, just hit him back harder, so he will never think of hitting you again.") A popular radio announcer in Toronto recalls running away from a bully as a child. When he ran home, his father pulled out a strap and told him to go back and fight the bully or face the strap at home. Girls are often taught to verbally abuse back. ("It takes one to know one.")

In all three of these encounters, someone can be seriously harmed, and most often it will be the target. Not true with the fourth level of defence:

4. Neither attacking nor provoking the attack, the target defends himself in such a way, and with such skill and control, that the attacker is not seriously harmed. The provoker may be on the ground if a physical move was used, yes, but will not be seriously harmed, as the target, once disempowering the bully, walks away from the confrontation. The chances of being targeted again are

slim. This is the ultimate in ethical self-defence. It is a skill that can be taught to children as young as six or seven. (Michael McMannis's dad gave Michael the tools to strike back with an assertive verbal response to Gorman's fist.)

At this fourth level, aikido involves both the *practical means* of self-defence and *ethical intention*. "The practice of the art of aikido then becomes a harmonious interaction between two or more people, fulfilling Master Uysehiba's intention via translation of the highest ethics of the East (and West as well) into vital and active modes of conduct." In other words, such harmonious interaction would benefit the bully, the bullied, and the bystander. As the authors noted at the end of their book, "If the student has accepted and is in agreement with the underlying principles of the art (restoration, reconciliation, harmony), he will endeavour to act in accordance with these principles by trying to apply these techniques as a means of neutralizing aggressions, not aggressors. Thus he achieves simultaneously the dual purpose of self-defence and restoration of that tenuous, living balance threatened by another man's temporary moral unbalance." This restoration is what is needed for your child and the child who bullied him to break out of the cycle of violence.

> It is the principle of the pure in heart never to injure
> others, even when they themselves have been hatefully
> injured. Hating others, even enemies who have harmed
> you unprovoked, assures incessant sorrow.
>
> —Ancient South Indian Scripture
> *Tirukkural* 32:312–13, sacred Tamil text

CHAPTER EIGHT

From Bystander to Witness

My doctrine is this, that if we see cruelty or wrong that we have the power to stop, and do nothing, we make ourselves sharers in the guilt.

—Anna Sewell,
Black Beauty

The one thing that doesn't abide by majority rule is a person's conscience.

—Harper Lee,
To Kill a Mockingbird

Chances are, if your son or daughter is not one of the two main characters—the bully or the bullied kid—he or she has been one of the supporting cast. Whom your child supported and how will affect not only the two main characters but your child as well.

Using the Bullying Circle on page 74, you can discuss with your children the roles they might have played, how they played them, and why. From there you can begin to teach them ways to move out of those roles, as well as counteract and prevent bullying in the future. Since much of the bullying goes on "under the radar" of adults, a potent force is kids themselves showing bullies that they will not be looked up to, nor will their cruel behaviour be condoned or tolerated.

If your child was a follower/henchman who took an active part but did not start the bullying, you can go through the same seven steps with him that you would with the child who was the bully (see page 114):

1. Intervene immediately with discipline.
2. Create opportunities to "do good".
3. Nurture empathy.
4. Teach friendship skills—assertive, respectful, and peaceful ways to relate to others.
5. Closely monitor your child's TV viewing, video game playing, computer activities, and music.
6. Engage in more constructive, entertaining, and energizing activities.
7. Teach your child to "will good".

To those steps you can add a dialogue with your child about ways to avoid being so easily led into doing the bidding of a more powerful peer. That involves two steps: figuring out how not to be so easily led, and hanging around kids who will not lead you down that path.

Ten-year-old David had joined in when a group of boys held down and took turns kicking nine-year-old Lewis. David's friend, Peter, tried unsuccessfully to pull him off the younger boy and then ran to get a teacher. David's mum was not only distressed by what her son had done but disturbed that he was not like Peter, who had refused to be a party to the abuse, had tried to keep his friend from getting involved, and had alerted a teacher. David said he just got caught up in the heat of the moment and even joined in calling Peter a "snitch", but he felt awful and wanted to get rid of the feeling. He had genuine remorse for his actions.

David's mum helped him go through the seven steps and explored his reasons and excuses for joining the bullying. As well, he apologized to Peter and thanked him for trying to stop him and for getting help. David invited both Lewis and Peter over for an evening of pizza and games. The two older boys agreed to buddy with the younger boy in the playground (see page 159 for more information on being a buddy).

She Hurt Her Through the Grapevine

Your daughter may not be happy about going through the three Rs—restitution, resolution, and reconciliation—if she was not the one to begin an ugly rumour. She merely repeated it. Nevertheless, she can:

1. apologize to the child who was harmed by the rumour;
2. go to everyone she told it to and tell them it wasn't true;
3. ask them to stop spreading it;
4. ask them to let everyone they told know that she was a part of spreading the rumour and wants to correct the damage done;
5. to the best of her ability, repair any harm done to the target by her act of spreading the rumour; and

6. heal with the child she harmed—invite the target of the rumour to join her for lunch, for a bike ride, to a sleepover.

You can encourage and support your daughter as she deals with the mixed responses from those with whom she shared the rumour. ("Thanks for telling me." "Wow, I spread it, too, what can I do?" "Look, you don't need to apologize for spreading a rumour—that kid is such a loser anyway." "Who is making you apologize?" "What are you doing? Trying to make the rest of us look bad?" "It was only a rumour. What's the big deal?" "You're no fun.") She will need your encouragement and support again as she faces the anger, hurt, and sadness that the targeted child will probably express. Throughout the whole process, your daughter will see not only the damage a rumour can cause, and how difficult—if not impossible—it is to repair, but also that she is capable of taking full responsibility for mistakes she has made.

Once she has gone through this process, you can talk with her about ways to effectively block a rumour in the future. The Sufis have a "wisdom saying" that our words must pass through three gates: *Is it true?* If it isn't, don't say it. If it is true, it must pass through two more gates before you speak it: *Is it necessary to say?* and *Is it kind?* If it is not necessary to say, don't speak it. If it is necessary, find a way to say it in a kind way. Kind does not mean candy-coating the truth; it means saying what needs to be said in a way that leaves the dignity and worth of all parties intact. ("Kim is such a wimpy loser" wouldn't make it through the first two gates. "Kim doesn't seem to know how to effectively stand up to those girls who are taunting her" passes through all three gates and opens the door for further discussion on how your daughter can be of help.)

By listening to the way your daughter speaks about the bully and her target, you may discern if she supported the bullying but did not take an active part, or if she liked the bullying but did not display open support at the time it occurred. ("Susan invited me to a sleepover. She didn't invite Kim. Everybody knows Kim is such a wimpy loser. Susan told everyone what a stupid thing Kim did at Jane's sleepover two weeks ago.") You can use this opportunity to talk to your daughter about the damage rumours can cause and encourage her to become a witness for Kim instead of a bystander. ("I'm uncomfortable talking about Kim behind her back. We don't have to like her; but we also don't have to spend our time ripping her apart.") Your daughter can also figure out ways to include Kim in social activities at school, such as inviting her to join her for lunch. In middle school, such an invitation may be a courageous act, as those who have selected Kim to be the target of their rumours and ostracism may shun your daughter. Talk to your daughter about enlisting one or two friends to join her in stopping the rumours and sitting with her at lunch. A bully may be more powerful than any one person but will not be more powerful than a committed group of witnesses.

There Are No Innocent Bystanders

If your son was a disengaged onlooker who watched a bunch of bullies rough up another boy and told you it was "none of my business; it happens all the time; I just ignore it", you can talk to him about the harm that silence can cause, not only to the targeted child but to him as well. Not to acknowledge bullying for what it is or to simply dismiss it is to still be a complicit bystander. When Elie Wiesel was asked, "What is the most important commandment in the Bible?" he said, "Thou shalt not stand idly by. The opposite of love is not hate, but indifference; indifference creates evil. Hatred is evil itself. Indifference is what allows evil to be strong, what gives it power." Your son's act of omission, although different from acts of commission by the other kids, can be addressed by going through the seven steps the followers/henchmen need to do to move from their respective roles to that of witness.

From henchman to disengaged onlooker, bystanders will often use the nine excuses discussed in Chapter Five for refusing to stand up and speak out against the bullying:

1. The bully is my friend.
2. It's not my problem! This is not my fight!
3. She is not my friend.
4. He's a loser.
5. He deserved to be bullied, asked for it, had it coming, so why stop it? He didn't even stand up for himself, so why should anyone else stand up for him?
6. Bullying will toughen him up.
7. Who wants to be called a snitch or a rat, blamed for getting someone else in trouble?
8. It's better to be in the in-group than to defend the outcasts.
9. It's too big a pain in the brain.

A bystander can weigh the pros and cons of remaining faithful to the group versus siding with the targeted kid. You can explain to your children how these excuses contribute to the overall erosion of civility in their peer group and increase the likelihood that they too will assume the role of bully. The erosion of civility could also cause your children to become targets for the bunches of bullies that would thrive in such an environment. You can assure your children that you know they are capable of moving out of the role of bystander. Stifling a bully requires a simple ethical principle: to do the right thing on behalf of a targeted peer, regardless of the actions of other bystanders.

Moving in the Right Direction

If your son or daughter is a possible defender—dislikes the bullying and would like to help out but doesn't, you can explore the four reasons kids may not help. They might:

1. be afraid of getting hurt;
2. be afraid of becoming a new target of the bully;
3. be afraid of doing something that will make the situation worse;
4. not know what to do.

If validated and talked about openly, these four reasons for remaining on the sidelines can be jumping-off points for helping kids become active witnesses—standing up for a peer, speaking out against an injustice, and taking responsibility for what happens among themselves. Talk with them about overestimating the comfort and safety of siding with the bully. Since the bully "uses" peers, your daughter could find herself on the wrong side of the bully for no other reason than that the bully decided to single her out next time, or your son could find himself in as much trouble as the bully when he becomes one of the "bunch of bullies".

You can discuss actions ranging from those that involve the least amount of risk on your children's part to those that require the greatest courage: from refusing to be a party to the bullying (moving away from the lunch table where kids are actively excluding others), to supporting the target privately ("That was a mean thing that he did to you; do you want to walk with us?"), to talking to the bully publicly or privately if she is a friend ("Leave her alone. Let's go get something to eat"), to intervening on behalf of the target, as Scott Russell and the football player did in the stories that follow. It might be as small a gesture as not repeating a rumour; inviting an isolated classmate to a sleepover; not laughing at a derogatory joke; offering kindness and concern to the target of a bully; telling an adult about the bullying; doing something riskier, such as joining with others to stand up to a bully; or stepping in alone. Indeed, as shown in the Toronto study (Pepler and Craig, 1995) that examined the roles of peers in bullying episodes observed in urban school playgrounds 13 percent of kids were willing to stand up and speak out. And they often did it in spite of the group, rather than within the safety of a group.

Willing Good

In Chapter Six, I discussed how a bully can take on a new role by "willing good"—that is, speaking and doing what is right "even when the burden is heavy". Helping your children develop an inner moral voice (personal code) that guides them to do or say what is right, often in spite of external consequences and never merely because of them, can give your children the strength to act with integrity when confronted with a bullying situation.

A fourth-generation Japanese-American and a highly successful conflict resolution consultant, Derek Okubo recalled an event that happened to him in the playground over thirty-five years ago. The only Japanese child in his class, he was surrounded by peers who beat him and called him names they had heard at home and in the classroom: "You little yellow Jap, go back where you came from." One boy, Scott Russell, came to his defence, took him away from the bunch of bullies, and invited Derek to join in a game. What Scott did at that moment demonstrated his own personal code. No slogans ("Celebrate diversity"), threats ("If you bully anyone, you will be suspended from school"), commands ("Don't call anyone else ugly names"), or even the Golden Rule ("Do unto others as you would have them do unto you") affected his decision so much as his own inner moral voice. Scott didn't come out of the womb knowing how to act with integrity. He had to learn it. He certainly didn't learn it in the playground.

Sad to say, he didn't learn it in the classroom, either. The incident in the playground came soon after Derek's teacher grabbed him by the shirt and yelled, "You get a 'U', you little yellow Jap," as Derek struggled with a "heel-to-toe, toe-to-heel, heel-together" activity in physical education class. Derek stood there stunned as his classmates watched this big man bully him verbally and physically. It's no wonder some of the kids felt comfortable attacking him in the playground. What was a big wonder to Derek is that one boy would be willing to stand up and speak out. As Derek told me his story some thirty-five years after the two incidents, he remarked that they had such an impact on his life that he could remember the activity he struggled with at the time, the words screamed at him both in the classroom and in the playground, and the full name of the boy who came to his aid.

Sharing, Caring, Helping, and Serving

In his book *Raising Your Child to Be a Mensch*, Neil Kurshan explains how kids like Scott learn to become witnesses: "Children do not magically learn morality, kindness, and decency any more than they learn maths, English, or science. They mature into decent and responsible people by emulating adults who are examples and models for them, especially courageous parents with principles and values who stand up for what they believe." It's important that our children see us stepping in, speaking up, and taking a stand against injustices, be those injustices in the family room, the boardroom, the classroom, or the city streets. When we do more than give lip service to our beliefs, when we walk our talk, we model for our children ways to be that potent force in stopping the bullying.

Preben Munch-Nielson, whom I wrote about in Chapter Four, was willing to rescue Jews in Denmark because "[y]ou just did. That's the way you were brought up". The majority of people in his community were willing to intervene on behalf of their neighbours. But our children must see us willing to stand up even when the rest of our neighbours are not. On March 2, 2002, in Ahmadabad, India, Virsing Rathod took such a stand. Beth Duff-Brown of the Associated Press wrote of his heroism:

> Horrified by the screams of his Muslim neighbours being beaten and burned alive, Virsing Rathod did what many other Hindus could not get up the courage to do.

The burly Hindu and his two sons jumped in a truck, rammed their way through frenzied Hindu rioters and began pulling Muslims from the flames just before midnight Thursday.

He saved 25 Muslims that night and has since sheltered dozens in safe houses across Ahmadabad, which is engulfed by Hindu-Muslim violence that has claimed 544 lives. . . . He shrugged when asked whether he's a hero.

"I did it out of humanity, because in my heart I knew it was the right thing to do."

How important it is for our children to see us stand by what we say, be accountable for it, and be willing to act on it—to do what is "the right thing to do".

Beyond *modelling*, we can give our children chances to *practise* being a witness. Rather than merely tell kids what to do or not to do, we can explain the whys of sharing, caring, helping, and serving and give kids the opportunity to do all four. They need to know that we care as much about their intent as we do about their actions. We can teach them to reflect on the impact of their actions on other people and be able to see things from another person's point of view. Once they can do that, they can begin to feel for the other person and put themselves in the other person's shoes. The ability to take another's perspective is crucial for "willing good". Not only was Scott able to take Derek's perspective and feel empathy with him, but Scott also had the courage to take the next step: "Hey, guys, back off, leave him alone." At this point Scott was choosing doing good over looking good to his classmates. Some kids may *want* to do something but are not able to withstand the peer pressure to conform. Scott was willing and able to withstand the sneers and jeers of his peers ("Jap lover") because he had a strong sense of self that had been nurtured by adults in his life.

Willing good involved taking a stand *and* taking action. It was not enough for Scott to feel Derek's pain. He needed to do something to alleviate it, even at the expense of alienating his friends. When Scott chose to step in "even when the burden was heavy", his words and actions gave others an opportunity and a way to at least opt out of the bullying, even if they were not ready to actively engage in doing the right thing. He also was teaching Derek an important lesson in tolerance. It was "white boys" who attacked him and a "white boy" who rescued him. The anger toward "white kids" that was beginning to boil inside Derek was cooled by the kindness and courage of one boy.

Taking a stand and taking action both require courage and moral independence. In their thought-provoking book, *Bringing Up a Moral Child*, psychologist Michael Schulman and school psychologist Eva Mekler write about the three principles that foster moral independence:

1. *Teach your child that he and only he is responsible for the consequences of his actions.* (Kids who accept responsibility for their own actions are more likely to live up to their own moral code—holding themselves accountable for their own behaviour and not blaming someone else.)
2. *Build your child's confidence in his or her ability to make good decisions.* (Kids who have confidence in their own judgments are not easily manipulated by others. They are not afraid to think and act independently.)
3. *Teach your child how to evaluate reasons on his or her own.*

(Kids who have confidence in their own ability to reason are more questioning and more resistant to passive acceptance of orders. They are able to evaluate whether or not an action is the right thing to do.)

The authors go on to mention a study, "Altruistic Behavior and the Parent–Child Relationship," by Dr Martin Hoffman. Dr Hoffman found that "parents who stress such 'altruistic' values as 'showing consideration of other people's feelings' and 'going out of one's way to help other people' were the ones most likely to have children who 'care about how other kids feel and try not to hurt their feelings', and who 'stick up for some kid that the other kids are making fun of or calling names' ".

Another Act of Kindness and Courage

Randy Binstock, a man who suffered through his school years with undiagnosed dyslexia, shared with me his story about the time he paid attention to the pain of a classmate and was willing to risk the scorn and assault of his peers to keep another teen from experiencing the humiliation he knew only too well.

"I was always picked on, from grade one till the end of high school. My best years were in kindergarten and grades one and two: they let us colour, which was great because I didn't have to speak. As I got older I was always made fun of because I couldn't read, and when the teacher asked me a question, I tried to turn myself into my favourite animal: the turtle. I thought if I could put my head into my shoulders she would never see me. Well, she did, and my classmates laughed at and made fun of me.

"One year at Dufferin Heights Secondary School, some boys

(a bunch of bullies) were picking on a big boy, Martin, who had a high voice. When they started beating him up I couldn't stand it any more and almost snapped. I told them they should stop beating him up and if they wanted they could beat me up instead. 'Where the hell did that come from?' I asked myself. I thought someone else had said it, but it was me. I got beat up. But you know, it was worth it because from that point on neither Martin nor I was ever beat up again. I got over the embarrassment of losing a fight and it didn't kill me.

"I've always taught my kids to be tolerant of everyone no matter how smart, stupid, fat, skinny, ugly, or just not able to communicate. There are usually a few things these people are able to do better than anyone in the world. I taught my kids that this is how we show love and respect for one another."

Randy's actions help demolish the myth that kids who are targeted for taunting—as he was repeatedly—are losers, worthless, inferior, or undeserving of respect. The opposite is more likely to be true. Targeted kids are often caring, compassionate, sensitive, creative, and thoughtful individuals.

Just as Scott could not stand by and let Derek be humiliated, so Randy was willing to take a risk for Martin. All four benefited from the small but not insignificant courageous acts of these two.

Becoming a Witness and Saving a Life

A Holocaust survivor listed the three actions to change a bystander into a witness: "Pay attention, get involved, and never ever look away." On October 17, 1996, a high-school football player did just that. For more than three months, members of a group known as Skaters terrorized a freshman, Josh, at Powell

High School in Powell, Tennessee. They mocked, taunted, and chased him, threatening to beat him to death with their chains and a baseball bat. Josh finally fought back, hitting one of the Skaters with a lunch tray, thinking that if he took on one of them, the bullying would stop. He was wrong. The two boys punched at each other, and Josh slipped and fell. As Josh lay on the floor unconscious, the other boy hit him in the head several times, shattering his skull. As other students looked on, a football player leapt over two tables and dragged Josh away, quite possibly saving his life.

If your children have been courageous enough to stand up to the bully and defend the targeted kid, you can thank them for acting courageously and talk to them about what they did, how they think the bullied child felt, how they felt themselves when they acted, and what more they can do. You may be inclined to think that your children should be "rewarded" for their courage. I would caution you to step back and reflect on the courageous act itself and the strong sense of satisfaction they felt by relieving the suffering of another child. An external reward can in fact "cheapen" the courageous act. (See Chapter Five for discussion on bribes and rewards.)

If your children are comfortable talking with you about the good, the bad, and the ugly, they will probably share with you the conflicted feelings they might have had before they acted on behalf of a bullied child—empathy, fear, sadness, or anger—and the discomfort they may have felt in going against the group. You can assure them that these feelings are normal and only reaffirm how courageous it was for them to step in and help a peer who was being harmed.

Sometimes it is a conscious act of disobedience when a child steps back, as Peter did, running to get help as the bully is giving marching orders to his henchmen. Or when Julie defied the orders (threats) Meridith dished out to her second-grade peers to go along with her story about Meghan pulling her trousers down in the playground and told her mum what really happened. Mark Twain's Huckleberry Finn committed a similar act of conscious disobedience in order to save a life. Sitting with a copy of the letter he wrote in which he told of the whereabouts of Jim, the slave he helped to escape, Huckleberry Finn struggled with feeling empathy and compassion for Jim, guilt over Jim's possible recapture thanks to the information in the letter, and fear of breaking the law and committing a grave sin—the state and the church having legal and moral injunctions against helping slaves escape. Tearing up the letter, Huckleberry says to himself, "All right then, I'll go to hell."

Taking the Risk of Telling an Adult

Even reporting a bullying incident to an adult can be a courageous act. The lesson about the differences between telling and tattling for a bullied kid is the same lesson you can teach your child (page 147). Once those ground rules—in trouble, don't tell; out of trouble, tell; and if it's both, I need to know—are understood, you can remind your children periodically that they can come to you with their concerns and fears. "You've heard it from me before, and you'll probably hear it from me again. If you are being bullied or if you know that someone else is being bullied, you need to report it to an adult you trust."

In *Steps to Respect*, the award-winning bullying prevention programme developed by the Committee for Children in the US, the authors teach elementary-school kids how to *recognize* bullying (Is it fair? How does it feel? Does it keep happening?); *refuse* bullying (Reject or say no to bullying behaviour); and *report* bullying (Anytime bullying is recognized it *can* be reported, but it *should* always be reported to an adult when "someone is unsafe; someone is touching or showing private body parts; or refusing the bullying doesn't work"). Along with the ground rules of "in trouble, out of trouble, or both", young kids can easily remember these three "should report" bullying situations. As a parent, you can play the "what if " game with your kids and help them role-play the witness—practising recognizing, refusing, and reporting. You are not only teaching your kids virtues you hold dear, you are helping them with the lines and actions for this all-important role. Aristotle summed up in four words the basics of teaching virtues to children: "Virtue is a habit."

Kids need to know you will treat the information seriously and confidentially (not disclose to the bully the source of your information) if necessary—but that you won't keep it a secret. Bullying thrives on secrecy. Kids have to trust that telling an adult will make a positive difference. Once they have shared the information with you, talk with them about what they can do and what you are going to do. If your son begs you not to get involved, hear him out and then share with him your concerns about the possible consequences of not acting and the possible actions you both can take—inaction is never an option when bullying is involved.

Younger children are more likely to tell an adult because they still believe an adult can and will do something that will make the bullying stop—not so with preteens and teenagers. Aside from the fact that they often believe adults will do nothing or that if they do, it will only make matters worse, adolescents are trying to find their own way in the world, without the interference of grown-ups. But the bullying experienced in high school often has far more devastating consequences for all parties involved, and appropriate adult intervention is usually necessary for serious bullying to be stopped. In the next chapter, we will look at how you and your children can work effectively with the school and the community to "recognize, refuse, report"—and respond.

A Pledge

Days after the shooting at Columbine High School in Littleton, Colorado, a group of Nashville, Tennessee, students created a website: www.iwillpledge.nashville.com. They invited other students throughout the world to sign the following pledge:

As part of my community and my school, I WILL:

- pledge to be a part of the solution.
- eliminate taunting from my own behaviour.
- encourage others to do the same.
- do my part to make my community a safe place by being more sensitive to others.
- set the example of a caring individual.
- eliminate profanity toward others from my language.
- not let my words or actions hurt others . . .

. . . and if others won't become a part of the solution, I WILL.

These kids were willing to take a leadership role, knowing that if they took a stand, others might follow. They also recognized that even if no one else followed in their footsteps, they would do what they knew was right.

> *Cowardice asks the question: is it safe?*
> *Expediency asks the question: is it politic?*
> *Vanity asks the question: is it popular?*
> *But conscience asks the question: is it right? And there comes a time when one must take a position that is neither safe, nor politic, nor popular—but one must take it because it's right.*

—Martin Luther King Jr

CHAPTER NINE

Caring Schools,
Involved Communities

Bully/victim problems in school really concern some of our basic values and principles. For a long time, I have argued that it is a fundamental democratic right for a child to feel safe in school and to be spared the oppression and repeated, intentional humiliation implied in bullying. No student should be afraid of going to school for fear of being harassed or degraded, and no parent should need to worry about such things happening to his or her child.

—Dr Dan Olweus in "Sweden",
The Nature of School Bullying:
A Cross-National Perspective

Since most instances of bullying occur in school-related settings, as a parent you will want to know what your child's school community is doing to make sure all students feel safe at school. Dr Dan Olweus, one of the leading international authorities on bullying, has developed a highly successful intervention programme in Bergen, Norway, that has proven to significantly reduce bullying in the schools that have adopted it. His programme is built on a set of four key principles: to create a school (and ideally also a home) environment characterized by:

1. warmth, positive interest, and involvement from adults;
2. firm limits as to unacceptable behaviour;
3. in case of violations of limits and rules, consistent application of non-hostile, non-physical sanctions (discipline as opposed to punishment);
4. behaviour by adults at home and at school that creates an authoritative (not authoritarian) adult-child interaction or child-rearing model.

These four principles translate into actions on an individual level, whole-class level, and schoolwide level in any number of ways. In his article "Health Consequences of Bullying and Its Prevention in Schools" (*Peer Harassment in Schools*), researcher Ken Rigby lists the elements commonly included in well-supported and effective antibullying policies:

1. A strong, positive statement of the school's desire to promote positive peer relations and especially to oppose bullying and harassment in any form it may take by *all* members of the school community.
2. A succinct definition of bullying or peer victimization, with specific examples.
3. A declaration of the right of individuals and groups in the school—students, teachers, other workers, and parents— to be free of victimization by others.

4. A statement of the responsibility of those who witness peer victimization to seek to stop it.
5. Encouragement of students and parents with concerns about victimization to speak with school personnel about them.
6. A general description of how the school proposes to deal with the bully/victim problem.
7. A plan to evaluate the policy in the near future.

Ask for a copy of your child's school's antibullying policy. [4] Check to see that it has the above four principles and seven elements necessary for an effective policy. In the end, you want to know that your child's school has a strong antibullying policy that is *clearly articulated, consistently enforced, and broadly communicated.* Along with the policy, you will want to be sure there are *procedures* and *programmes* that back up and reinforce the policy as well as create a safe and caring environment for students. It is one thing to have a policy; it is wholly another to make sure the policy is not just placards on the school wall or an inspirational piece of writing at the beginning of the student handbook. It is the school culture and social environment that these policies, procedures, and programmes create as well as reflect.

One project that includes all three—policy, procedures, and programme—is the critically acclaimed *Steps to Respect* developed by the Committee for Children (www.cfchildren.org). *Steps to Respect* is based on Dr Olweus's model and is used in elementary schools in the United States and Canada. It is a

---

[4] In the UK, head teachers in all schools must by law have an written policy to prevent all forms of bullying among pupils. This policy must comply with the Human Rights Act 1998. *Bullying—Don't Suffer in Silence*, issued by the Department for Education and Skills on behalf of the British government, provides guidance on formulating the policy and choosing strategies for reducing bullying. All schools must have a governors' statement on how children should behave, and the school's discipline policy and any school rules must be based on this statement. The head teacher must tell parents about the rules each year.

prevention programme designed not only to decrease bullying, but also to help students build more supportive relationships with one another. It teaches skills for coping with bullying, including recognizing bullying, using assertive behaviours to refuse bullying, and reporting bullying to adults. It is one of the few programmes that addresses the critical role of the bystander and emphasizes the responsibility of all members of the school community to decrease bullying. Lessons in the various units teach empathy for targets of bullying and specific helpful ways children can respond when they witness bullying. It also emphasizes the adults' crucial role: "Bullying can be a seriously destructive element in relationships among children at school, among adults in the workplace, and within families. The school setting provides educators with the opportunity to teach children that bullying is wrong—and that there are positive ways of influencing others. Through the lessons they teach in class and their actions in the playground, adults can demonstrate the power of caring, respectful, and responsible citizenry." Following the prevention strategies that have received scientific support in studies done by Dr Olweus and others respected in the field, *Steps to Respect* recommends for optimal intervention the following schoolwide components:

1. **Gathering information about bullying at school directly from students.** This would involve first increasing awareness among students, educators, and parents as to the definition of bullying, the three kinds of bullying— verbal, physical, and relational—and the roles students can and do play (see the Bullying Circle on page 74). Second, it entails surveying anonymously students, educators, and

parents about the nature and quality of peer relations at the school. Don't be surprised if students report more incidents of bullying than parents or educators suspect. Third, it is necessary to ask kids what they need from adults in order to feel safe.

2. **Establishing clear schoolwide and classroom rules about bullying.** Kids need to know what the rules are, that they will be enforced, and how they will be enforced. It is important that the constructive consequences require that those partaking in the bullying go through the three Rs: restitution, resolution, and reconciliation. There also needs to be a plan of action if the intervention does not work and the bully does not change his or her behaviour. This plan can include removal from a class or school and a referral to another programme such as an alternative school, a mental health agency, or the police. Along with the rules, the school needs to create strong social norms against bullying, with programmes to prevent, identify, and combat bullying.

3. **Training all adults in the school to respond sensitively and consistently to bullying.** Bullied kids want to know that they will be supported and protected and that adults will take responsibility for the safety of all students. Educators should teach tolerance and diversity awareness and model positive, respectful, and supportive behaviours. No longer will "kids will be kids", "it's his own fault, he was asking for it", or "they were just teasing" work as excuses by educators for not intervening.

4. **Providing adequate adult supervision, particularly in less structured areas, such as in the playground and in the**

lunchroom. Students want a greater adult presence in all areas of the school as well as on the school bus. One of the most effective strategies to make a school safe is the physical presence of responsible adults.

5. **Improving parental awareness of and involvement in working on the problem.** You as a parent can model positive, respectful, and supportive behaviours; help your children develop a strong sense of self; teach them how to make friends; and teach them how to become a part of a group. You can teach them to relate to others in a positive and respectful way, to be assertive, and to stand up and speak out against injustices.

You can volunteer to help create a greater presence of caring adults in the school, work with educators to make sure policies are implemented, and serve as an advocate for your child.

You can lobby your school board or board of trustees for adequate funding for additional staff needed for supervision, for support services, and for programmes that can back up the strong policies and rules and consequences that states and provinces are mandating. Severe cutbacks in funding in both the United States and Canada have undermined the safety of students. Boards have eliminated supervisory functions teachers used to perform; hall monitors are almost nonexistent; there are few, if any, lunchroom monitors left, fewer educational assistants and guidance counsellors—all critical elements for the safety and well-being of students.

Find out what kind of communication will be forthcoming from the school if your child is bullying or being bullied—phone, letter, note—and what procedures you can follow if you are concerned about a bullying situation that school personnel may not know about yet.[5]

Kids can't stop the bullying they experience or witness all by themselves. They need adults at home, in the school, and in community programmes committed to breaking this cycle of violence wherever they see it and whenever they hear about it.

In my research for this book, I was unable to find any such comprehensive programme for middle school and high school in either the United States or Canada. Following are two programmes I researched that address preventing teen violence and have proven track records in schools that have implemented their programmes:

1. *Safe Teen: A Life-Skills and Violence Prevention Programme* (www.safeteen.ca) by Anita Roberts of Vancouver, British Columbia, offers an in-depth look at issues and skills such as:

   - how to access inner strength and form healthy relationships.
   - the importance of building and respecting boundaries.
   - how to deal with bullying and sexual harassment.
   - the importance of embracing differences and

---

[5] In the UK, if your child is being bullied, you could first ask to speak to the class teacher with your child. If you need to take the matter further, arrange a meeting with the head or deputy head teacher. The next step would be to write formally to the Board of Governors (School Boards in Scotland). If you feel strongly that the school is turning its back on the problem, you can approach the Director of Education for the local authority. In serious cases, the school might be judged legally responsible if the teachers have not stopped bullying, spoken or physical, that has caused a child serious harm.

understanding the roots of racism, sexism, and homophobia.

- how to make wise choices about personal safety, drugs, and alcohol.

Anita Roberts has also written a book, *Safe Teen: Powerful Alternatives to Violence*, which both teens and their parents can read for ways teens can deal with peer pressure, de-escalate violence, and develop a strong sense of self.

2. *Personal and Social Responsibility* and *Mastering Anger* is a two-part curriculum series for middle-school and high-school students (www.iasd.com) developed by Constance Dembrowsky of the Institute for Affective Skills Development of La Luz, New Mexico. These courses address:

- developing self-discipline.
- identifying consequences before taking action.
- recognizing the impact of the student's actions on others.
- getting what the student wants in ways that maintain dignity and respect for himself and possibly others.
- mastering anger, not surrendering to it.
- resolving conflicts peacefully.

These two courses can be taught sequentially or can stand alone. Both courses include materials for optional parent training sessions.

As a parent, you may want to be involved with your school's research into these and other programmes that can help create a school climate that supports creative, constructive, and responsible activities and work toward reducing all forms of violence, including bullying.

Bullying happens in every school. You want to be sure that your child's school is proactive and deals with all three kinds of bullying—physical, verbal, and relational—promptly, firmly, and consistently. Educators need to be vigilant in addressing all incidents of bullying. If your child's school does not have an antibullying policy with procedures and programmes to back up the policy, you may find yourself in the same spot Hoss's mum found herself in when her son's teacher saw the bullying as the bullied kid's problem.

Nicknamed Hoss by his family when he was a toddler, five-year-old Howard was subjected to unmerciful taunting by a small group of boys in the playground. His teacher called his mum and suggested that in order to eliminate their favourite taunt, "Hossy Bossy", Hoss should start going by his given name of Howard. Not seeing how changing his name would stop the taunting, Hoss's mum retorted, "Why? So they can call him Howard the Coward instead?" A more satisfactory solution would be to deal with the tormentors directly. But it is not uncommon that the situation is viewed as the target's problem to solve alone. Targets of bullies often elicit little empathy from classmates and adults. You may have to be persistent in your insistence that bullying be addressed at its source—the bully. There will be times when you may have to help your bullied child work on behaviours that get in the way of healthy relationships with peers, but nobody ever deserves to be bullied. If you are concerned about the teacher's proposed solution or lack of response, know that you can go to that teacher's supervisor or to the principal, as Sophie's mother did.

Twelve-year-old Sophie, who had a hearing impairment, was being taunted by her classmates out of sight and earshot of her teacher. When the taunting became unbearable, Sophie told her mum. Mum and daughter had a meeting with the teacher— Sophie's mum being there as a support while Sophie talked about the incidents. The teacher expressed sympathy, then shrugged and said, "That's just how girls this age behave." Worse, she began to list all the things she thought Sophie was doing that brought on the ugly name-calling and suggested that if she weren't such a wimp, this wouldn't be happening. Fortunately for Sophie, her mum didn't stop with this one meeting. She informed the teacher that she felt the bullying was not normal, nor should her daughter or any other child have to tolerate such meanness. The next step was a meeting with the principal and this teacher. The principal agreed with Sophie's mum, promptly dealt with the bully and her followers, supported Sophie, and required the teacher to attend a workshop entitled "Dealing Effectively with Bullying".

Beware: Zero Tolerance Can Equal Zero Thinking

At the opposite end of the continuum, all fifty states and most Canadian provinces, as well as the three Canadian territories, have instituted zero-tolerance policies against bullying and other forms of violence as well as against possession of weapons and use of drugs. The intent of these policies is laudable, but the singular procedure—one size fits all (that is, mandatory suspension or expulsion)—that many school districts have implemented is inflexible, harsh, and lacking in common sense. [6] It requires an "all or nothing" approach that gives administrators the message "You have no choice" and has resulted in a reckless and punitive approach that has an overtone of vindictiveness and has also brought increased lawsuits against schools regarding unfairness and inequities. Some examples of zero tolerance in less than effective action:

- A first-grader suspended for three days for pointing a breaded chicken finger at a friend like a gun.
- Two eight-year-olds arrested and charged with "making terrorist threats" for wielding a paper gun in class.
- A thirteen-year-old boy expelled for making a list of his enemies, which a classmate found in the trash and showed to a teacher.
- An eleven-year-old arrested for having a plastic knife in her lunchbox to cut chicken.
- A ten-year-old expelled for "possession of a lethal weapon" after she voluntarily turned in a small knife she found in her lunch sack. The girl had picked up her mum's lunch sack instead of her own. The small knife was to cut an apple. The teacher thanked the girl for doing the right thing; the principal promptly suspended the girl because there was "no leeway in the law".
- A six-year-old accused of "sexual harassment" for running out of the bath in his own home to tell the school bus driver to wait for him.

---

[6] In the UK, it is the head teacher who may exclude (expel) a child for a fixed period of time or permanently. Physical punishment is illegal in all schools, although "reasonable force" may be used to stop a child committing a crime, hurting someone or damaging something. If a school wants to exclude your child, you can write to the school's Board of Governors telling them why you think your child shouldn't be excluded. If the governors agree with the head teacher's decision, you can appeal to an independent appeal panel set up by the local education authority.

- A sixteen-year-old expelled after he turned in an English assignment in which he wrote about his thoughts of getting revenge on those students who had taunted and physically harassed him daily.

In March 2001, the American Bar Association released a statement opposing such zero-tolerance procedures, calling them a "one size fits all solution to all the problems that schools confront. It redefined students as criminals, with unfortunate consequences".

An antibullying policy that has zero tolerance for bullying is a good thing. No one wants his child bullied at school. What is needed are procedures to support that policy that provide opportunities for administrators to exercise fairness, common sense, and sound discretion. All bullying should have some sanction. It doesn't mean you apply the maximum sanction for every offense.

At San Marcos High School in San Marcos, California, a student drew up a list of his tormentors on the back of a class handout. Parents of some of the students on the list insisted that the principal do something. Principal Frans Weits did what they demanded, but not in the way they expected. She ordered an investigation. Students were asked what they had done to their classmate that would merit getting their name on his list. She then called to account everyone involved in the incident—bullies, henchmen, active supporters to disengaged onlooker, and the bullied boy who wrote the list. The principal was quoted in the local newspaper: "In light of what's happened in neighboring districts, San Marcos High now has a zero-tolerance policy toward bullying. And everyone—faculty, staff, students and parents—is on notice that students will be held accountable for everything from verbal harassment to physical aggression" (*San Diego Tribune*, April 14, 2001). San Marcos had a policy, procedures, and a committed administrator who was willing to follow through in order to create a safe school community for all of the students. The zero-tolerance policy in that district was accompanied by procedures that allowed for the exercise of fairness and common sense as well as sound discretion and judgment on the part of the administrator. Each student had to take responsibility for his or her own behaviour and go through disciplinary procedures that were, as Dan Olweus suggests, "non-hostile, non-physical sanctions".

One of the neighbouring districts the principal referred to was Sante, California, where weeks before, a boy whose cries went unheard, whose pain was ignored, and whose oppression went unabated and unrelieved struck back with a vengeance, killing two schoolmates and wounding thirteen more, as well as several adults. In other districts across both Canada and the United States, kids, feeling they have no other way out of the pain and torture heaped on them by their tormentors, no one to turn to, and no one to tell, kill themselves. In their book, *Bullycide*, Neil Marr and Tim Field point an accusing finger at those who do not do what principal Frans Weits saw as critical: "Each bullycide is an unpalatable fact that a child has died as a result of the deliberate actions of another in an environment where the responsible adults have failed to provide a mechanism for reporting, intervening, and dealing with physical and psychological violence. The excuses of 'we didn't know' or 'we didn't understand' are no longer valid."

School Climate and Culture

Along with an antibullying policy and procedures, check to see that your school has programmes that actually work toward changing the climate and culture of a school.

Most educators want "to do the right thing" and stop hurtful behaviour, says Arthur Coleman, deputy assistant secretary in the US Department of Education's Office for Civil Rights. Coleman was part of a team that created "Protecting Students from Harassment and Hate Crime: A Guide for Schools". (The full text is available on-line at www.ed.gov/pubs/Harassment.) The guide emphasizes that schools take a comprehensive approach such as developing written policies that prohibit harassment and instituting a formal complaint policy. In an interview for ASCD (Association for Supervision and Curriculum Development) Curriculum Update Fall 1999, the authors of the guide explain, "We want to help educators look for ways to be proactive and strategic on the front end to avoid heartbreak on the back end." They also note, "[W]ritten anti-harassment policies and complaint procedures will not stop or prevent harassment." In the same update, Terrence Deal, Irving R. Melbo Professor of Education, University of California, agreed, "In and of themselves, policies and procedures, rules and regulations, often serve as substitutes for values—they hang on the wall and not in people's heads and hearts. What schools need is that shared sense of 'this is the way we do things here'."

Written by Steve Seskin and Allen Shamblin and made famous by Peter, Paul and Mary, the song "Don't Laugh at Me" (Chapter Three) serves as the theme for the critically acclaimed project Operation Respect: Don't Laugh at Me (www.dontlaugh.org).

Founder and director Peter Yarrow developed this programme, available free to schools that want to create "safe and caring climates in which children learn to treat each other with respect". In the fact sheet accompanying the programme, Peter Yarrow reiterates the need for that shared sense of "This is the way we do things here": "Let's not wait to fix our children after the fact any more. Let's not wait for the good-spirited, open, malleable clay of young children to become hardened. Though we must address the needs of all children with equal passion, let's not just focus on those who have become troubled and potentially dangerous to themselves and to others. Let us work proactively together to help evolve a next generation of whole, caring, confident, and productive citizens."

In their book *Peacemakers*, Roger and David Johnson write of the importance of the education of the whole child, of tending to children's social and emotional development as well as to their academic growth: "While schools teach math, reading, social studies, and science, perhaps the most important thing for students to learn is how to interact effectively and peacefully with each other and the world at large." Whether your child is the bully, the one bullied, or a potential bystander, your active participation in the school community can help assure that there is a shared sense of "This is the way we do things here"—at home, in school, and in the community—that the needs of all children are addressed with "equal passion", and that your child and her classmates learn to "interact effectively and peacefully". Your involvement can range from volunteering in the classroom or helping supervize open areas of the school (high school included) to participating in the parent-student-teacher organization active in your child's school or assisting in club activities. Once again, the key to dealing effectively with bullying is to "pay attention, get involved, and never ever look away".

Planned intervention in our schools can greatly reduce bullying and its subsequent negative impact on individual children, the school community, and the entire community. Research has shown that bullying can be reduced if educators, students, and parents work together to create a climate in which there is an *esprit de corps*—the spirit of devotion and enthusiasm among members of a group for one another, their group, and their purpose—and in which all kids believe they have worth, are capable human beings, are expected to serve, and can resolve conflicts nonviolently. In middle schools and high schools, however, there is a major cultural obstacle to this *esprit de corps*—cliques.

Cliques

In the movie *The Breakfast Club*, five students at a high school with a rigid social system were assigned to Saturday suspension for a variety of "crimes" they committed. Each student was assigned to compose an essay telling who they thought they were. Instead they spent the day in a series of adventures that allowed them to go beyond their facades, their pretenses, and their roles and come to know one another as human beings—more alike than different and more caring than "cool". The final essay, composed and read by one of the teenagers, but submitted to the vice principal on behalf of all five, rails against the rigid social system that was artificially created and followed blindly until that fateful Saturday:

Dear Mr. Bernard,

We accept the fact we had to sacrifice a whole Saturday in detention for whatever it was that we did wrong. What we did was wrong. But we think you're crazy to make us write an essay telling you who we think we are. What do you care? You see us as you want to, in the simplest terms and the most convenient definitions. You see us as a brain, an athlete, a basket case, a princess, and a criminal, correct? That's the way we saw each other at seven o'clock this morning. We were brainwashed. But what we found out is that each one of us is a brain, an athlete, a basket case, princess, and criminal. Does that answer your question?

Sincerely yours,
The Breakfast Club

In his book *Nobody Left to Hate: Teaching Compassion After Columbine*, Elliot Aronson wrote about this poisonous atmosphere in middle and senior high school, which he saw as one of the root causes of violence:

It's the cliquish atmosphere of rejection and humiliation that makes a very significant minority of students; I would say 30 to 40 percent of them, very, very unhappy. If kids at the top of the pyramid start calling a kid a nerd, then the kids in the second tier of cliques tease him because that's one way of identifying with the powerful group. The next thing you know, everybody's teasing him. Everybody in school knows what group everybody belongs to. They know whom they can get away with taunting.

It is reasonably clear that a major root cause of the

recent school shootings is a school atmosphere that ignores, or implicitly condones, the taunting, the rejection, and verbal abuse to which a great many students are subjected. A school that ignores the values of empathy, tolerance, and compassion—or, worse still, pays lip service to these values while doing nothing concrete and effective to promote these values—creates an atmosphere that is not only unpleasant for the "losers," but one that short-changes the "winners" as well.

Eric Harris and Dylan Klebold wrote about the resentment they had for the caste system, where popular athletes were accorded star status at their school. After the shootings at Columbine, other students voiced similar concerns about the hierarchy of cliques perpetuated by students and tolerated by administrators. Evan Ramsey, at the bottom of the rigid social system of his small high school in Alaska, was the target of abuse for years. Alexandra Shea wrote of the "junior capos who run the social underground". The kids from The Breakfast Club found a way for kids from various backgrounds to begin to accept one another not as the same, but as uniquely different, each with gifts and talents and foibles to bring to the table—and to projects (granted, some of the projects the Breakfast Club engaged in would not be ones you want to encourage, but it was the working and sharing and being human in front of one another that began to break down the prejudices, stereotypes, and bigotry they originally held).

The more opportunities students from diverse backgrounds and interests have to work and play together, the less likely they will be to form cliques that have as their hallmark exclusion and derision of those "beneath" them. The more administrators and other adults in the school as well as in the community refuse to elevate one group over all the others—with all the accompanying privileges—the less likely it will be that these groups will have the notion that they can bully someone who is not a part of their "elite" group. No small task, I know, to dismantle the social caste systems in our middle schools and high schools, but I agree with Elliot Aronson that to tackle bullying, we must tackle its root causes—and a rigid social system of cliques is one of those causes. To establish an antibullying policy and at the same time condone a poisonous social environment that implicitly supports social stratification and social privilege, which in turn results in injustice, oppression, subjugation, and humiliation, is to be silently complicit in fuelling the rage of those at the bottom of the heap.

Been Bullied

Whether your child tells you about being bullied, your child's best friend's parent breaks the news to you, or you find a note dropped in the back seat of the car detailing the ugly incidents, after you have talked with your child (Chapter Seven), you will want to let her teachers know about the bullying she is experiencing at school. There are five steps to take:

1. Arrange a meeting for you and your child with the appropriate person at the school. If your school has an antibullying policy and procedures in place, there may be a specific person in the building assigned and trained to intervene effectively. It is important that your son or

daughter who was bullied be an important part of finding a solution to the problem of the bullying. If all the adults get together to talk about a solution without the child being actively involved, the child is even further disempowered. If your child is a teenager, she can take the lead at this initial meeting, with you as her support.

2. Bring to the meeting the facts in writing—the date, time, place, kids involved, and the specifics of the incidents— and the impact the bullying has had on your child as well as what your child has done to try to stop the bullying that didn't work. (Putting everything in writing beforehand will help you and your child effectively present the facts that could be forgotten if you both rely on memory in what could be an emotionally charged meeting.)

3. Work with your child and school personnel on a plan that addresses what your child needs right now in order to feel safe, what she can do to avoid being bullied and to stand up to any future bullying, and whom she can go to for help. The plan will also include what the adults are going to do to keep her and other potential targets safe and stop further bullying.

4. Find out what procedures the bully will be going through and what kind of support the school is expecting from the parents of the bully. At this point, you can discuss the possibility of your child and the bully meeting *at a later date* for the third step in the discipline process— reconciliation. No one is likely to see this as an option right now, but let the school know that you feel it is important that the healing take place if possible *after* the bully (or bullies) has gone through the other steps. Set a time to

review the plan with the appropriate school personnel.

5. If you feel the problem is not being adequately addressed by the school, know that you can express your concerns and let the teacher and/or administrator know that you will take the next step to the school district board office and if necessary—especially in cases of serious abuse or racist or sexist bullying—to the police (in the United States, you can contact the US Department of Education Office for Civil Rights (OCR), which can often initiate legal action against the bully or the school board). Schools are responsible for protecting students and are culpable when they don't.[7]

To Change or Not to Change

Your child has a right to be educated in an environment that is free of fear and harassment. Your child is likely to need a lot of support if he has been bullied for a length of time. Know that he may be in shock, physically and emotionally harmed, fearful that the bullying will happen again, incredibly sad, and just plain unwilling to trust the kid (or bunch of kids) who bullied him. His thoughts may have turned to revenge, his feelings to rage. To help him begin to heal, you will need to create for him an atmosphere of compassion, kindness, gentleness, and patience and provide a safe and secure environment. Ideally, that environment would include your child's school, where the adults treat bullying as a serious matter and respond sensitively and effectively to your child's report; where the bully is required to go through the process of reconciliatory justice, and where peers are respectful and friendly toward your child.

---

7 See footnote to page 201.

I am not a strong proponent of moving the target of bullying to another classroom or school to get away from the bullying. Two things can happen: The bullying continues at the first school; and the target—without proper support and intervention—will be in a weakened state and an even more vulnerable target at the new school. But sometimes a move, with support and intervention, may be the best solution for your child. It was for Rachel, the girl mentioned in Chapter Three, who, after suffering five and a half years of bullying, moved to a new school and thrived as she was "treated like a human again". I agree with Judith Rich Harris, author of *The Nurture Assumption*, who wrote, "If my kid were at the very bottom of the local totem pole, and if all the higher-ups were beating on him, I would want to get him out of there. Victims are victimized partly because they get a reputation for being victimizable, and it is extremely difficult to change the peer group's mind about things like that. Usually moving is a disadvantage for a kid because he loses his peer group and whatever status he had in it. But if the peer group is making his life miserable and his status is zero, he doesn't have much to lose."

The decision to change or not change a child's classroom or school is not a simple or easy one. Ken Rigby's seven elements for an effective antibullying policy and the five schoolwide components listed in *Steps to Respect* can help you identify a school in which your child can thrive. These elements and components, combined with your knowledge of your child, as well as his own input, can help you choose the best option. Running away is not a solution, but sometimes moving to a more caring classroom or school is the best one.

A Bully on the Home Front

If it is your child who is doing the bullying, be he the main character or a henchman of the bully, the phone call from the school may leave you sad, angry, frustrated, and disappointed. It is important that you listen and not try to justify, rationalize, minimize, or make excuses for your child's bullying. ("The other boy must have asked for it." "Everyone calls everyone else names like that. Why are you picking on my son?" "He was just teasing." "His father and I are getting a divorce. It's not his fault that he is acting that way.") To get the most constructive outcome, Ted Feinburg of the National Association of School Psychologists recommends:

1. Strive to be nondefensive. You want to hear the school's concerns.
2. Ask exactly what happened. Try not to react emotionally.
3. Ask what the school has done to remedy the problem.
4. Ask your child what happened. (See Chapter Six, "Is There a Bully in the House?")
5. If a meeting is scheduled to deal with the problem, make sure you understand the agenda. Write down any concerns you have about how the school is dealing with your child.
6. If your child acts differently at home, or if there are discipline strategies that have worked for you, tell the school official.
7. Work with the school to solve the problem. Make clear that you're an ally here and that you trust the school will act as an ally.

If you try to rescue your son or blame your son's target, you run the risk of shutting down any constructive communication and inviting defensiveness on the part of school personnel. As well, you are sending your son the message that you sanction his bullying. If the school uses punishment (suspension) instead of discipline, you can act as an advocate for both your son and for the child your son bullied by suggesting a plan that incorporates the seven steps discussed in Chapter Six:

1. Intervene immediately with discipline.
2. Create opportunities to "do good".
3. Nurture empathy.
4. Teach friendship skills—assertive, respectful, and peaceful ways to relate to others.
5. Closely monitor your child's TV viewing, video game playing, computer activities, and music.
6. Engage in more constructive, entertaining, and energizing activities.
7. Teach your child to "will good".

Your son may still be suspended, but the suspension can be used constructively to fix what he did (restitution), figure out how he is going to keep it from happening again (resolution), and come up with a plan to heal with the child he has harmed (reconciliation). As an educator, I always welcomed ideas from parents who wanted to be a part of the solution, were willing to listen, and were open to suggestions from those of us who were with their children five hours a day.

You can discuss ways you will help your son do the seven steps and suggest how the educators working with your son can help.

For instance, your son may be able to "do good" by reading to second-graders or helping out in the library.

When Bullying Becomes a Crime

If your teenager's bullying has caused serious injury, irrevocable harm, or death (or if it was your child who was seriously harmed), you may find it helpful to remember how families and communities around the world have used reconciliatory justice in the aftermath of such violence. Reconciliatory justice is a visible expression of forgiveness and the act of healing in a community. It is perhaps the one tool that can begin to cut through the chains of violence. It does not excuse the violence, and it does not deny the dignity and worth of the victim or the humanity of the bully. It does justice to the suffering without perpetuating the hatred. It is a triumph of mindfulness and compassion over vengeance and retribution. Reconciliatory justice is not about punishment; it's about maintaining human connections.

During the process, we hold out two hands to the bully—one of restraint, the other of compassion. The first hand keeps the bully from causing more harm to himself or to others; the second hand offers compassion to the bully, allows time for reflection, and invites reconciliation. As our two hands reach out, there is at once an attempt to bring about balance and a tension created that keeps both parties actively engaged in the reconciliatory process, as we strive to heal the rift created. We are attempting to restore community. The end goal is an embrace in which the bully takes responsibility as is warranted, is willing to make restitution, resolves to keep the bullying from happening again, and commits to once again becoming an active participant in the community. In that embrace, we are ready and willing to have him as a participating member of our community.

In April of 2002, the teenager who was convicted of threatening and harassing fourteen-year-old Dawn Marie Wesley before she committed suicide agreed to participate in an aboriginal healing circle with Dawn Marie's family to determine what her sentence would be. The dead girl's mother suggested that the healing circle be used because she was frustrated with the traditional justice system that didn't allow the families of the offender and the victims to communicate. Any sentence imposed by the healing circle will include actions that will invite healing and restoration. A First Nations elder and author Ovid Mercredi writes in the book *In the Rapids*, "We use elders to deal with the source of the problems, not just the symptoms, and to correct the imbalance in the community by healing both the victims and the offenders. The focus is on healing and restoration, not the adversarial process and punishment . . . decisions would be rendered from the perspective of healing, compensation, and reconciliation as opposed to . . . punishment, deterrence, and imprisonment."

In *No Future Without Forgiveness*, Archbishop Desmond Tutu wrote about this same kind of justice, "We contend that there is another kind of justice, restorative justice, which is characteristic of traditional African jurisprudence. Here the central concern is not retribution or punishment. In the spirit of *ubuntu* the central concern is the healing of breaches, the redressing of imbalances, the restoration of broken relationships."

If creating more caring, more compassionate, less alienating, less violent communities is a goal, we must give up our desire for swift revenge and retribution, stronger punishments and stiffer sentences. When the main goal is to make children "pay dearly" for what they have done and serve as examples for others who might think of doing the same, hate and bitterness find rich soil in which to grow. How bullies are treated will influence what kind of people they will grow up to be and what kinds of lives the rest of us will live. If we don't help them reconcile with the community, we could well condemn ourselves to a lifetime of fear, distrust, and mayhem.

When an entire community is committed to reconciliatory justice, bullies are invited to rise above their misdeeds and violent acts. The goal is to mend and restore rather than isolate and punish. The search is not for vengeance, but for ways to heal people and relationships.

A Community Incident That Involved the School

A thirteen-year-old boy was attacked by five peers at a sleepover at a classmate's home. He was taunted, then jumped on and slammed into furniture. He ended up with cuts and severe bruises that were documented by a doctor and police the next day. Too afraid to call home, he stayed the night and participated the next day in the school activity the boys were supposedly preparing for at the sleepover. During that day, he tried desperately not to call attention to himself. It was only when his mum picked him up from school that he broke down and told her about what his classmates had done the night before.

The school administrators decided to mount their own investigation side by side with the police and said that they were appalled that such a violent incident could occur among classmates at a private religious school. Their comment: "We will take steps to see that if it did occur, it won't again. The safety and well-being of our students is our top priority." It may have been a top priority—good policy—but there were no procedures in place to protect the bullied child. He returned to school after taking one day off. But the boys who beat him were now bragging about the attack and said they would "do worse if he didn't shut up about the incident". The thirteen-year-old then stayed home the rest of the week. (When procedures are not in place to immediately provide safety for the target and put some kind of restraint on the bullies—be it closer supervision, alterations to their schedule, or temporary exclusion—it is the bullied child who suffers once again by missing school out of fear of further bullying.)

Many of the older kids called the bullied boy and offered support and protection—true witnesses instead of bystanders.

His parents sent out letters to all of the parents in their son's class. None of the families of the bullies responded or apologized after receiving the letters. Frustrated by the lack of response by the parents of the bullies, the parents of the bullied child filed charges against the bullies, hoping the charges would convince the bullies and their parents of the seriousness of the incident.

Once it moves into legal territory, an adversarial situation will probably develop whereby neither side will be able to talk with the other or reach any kind of reconciliation. This was the same frustration that Dawn Marie's mother experienced as sides were drawn up and animosity grew. Consider the contrast if all of the parties agreed to some kind of healing circle. In the healing circle, each boy would be able to admit his own part in the incident and develop a plan for fixing what he did, figuring out how to keep it from happening again, and healing with the boy who was bullied.

In such a setting, the main bully would have a different problem and thus a different plan and follow-up from the boy who joined in willingly, or the one who joined reluctantly but joined nevertheless, or the one who hung back, too scared to do anything but watch.

Such a circle can involve school personnel at all stages of the healing process, assessing meaningful consequences for each boy, following up on their plans to keep it from happening again, and—as the main social setting where they all spend the most time—encouraging activities to heal the rift and thus heal as a school community.

A Bully in the Backyard

What do you do when the bully is right in your backyard, terrorizing your children and their peers who gather in your yard to play? It is important that you distinguish between the usual hassles, disagreements, and conflicts all kids engage in with one another and actual bullying. Kids themselves can handle most squabbles, and they should be encouraged to do so. But if it is bullying, you will want to intervene. It is helpful to both the bully and the bullied child if you can use the same steps you would have used if it was one of your children twisting your other child's arm behind his back (page 110). You can also appeal to the better side of the child's nature and invite her to do something helpful. "You are so strong, can you help me move this planter away from the sandbox?" As she is helping you, you can tell her how she is misusing her leadership skills and how she can use those skills in a better way. And make it a point to hang around within view and earshot of the group as they continue to play. As with schools, one of the easiest ways to ensure safety for kids is the physical presence of responsible adults.

If it is serious bullying and you are unable to get the bully to see the error of her ways, you may have to ask her to go home. If the situation happened at school, I recommend that you not call the parents directly, but let the school act as an intermediary. In this case and other situations in your neighbourhood, you may have to go it alone. When you call the bully's parent, just as you appealed to the better side of the bully's nature, you can appeal to her parent's better side as well. "I would like very much for your daughter and mine to play together. Today, an incident happened that I know you will want to know about. Can we get together and talk about it with both of the girls? It is important to me that our girls be able to play together."

The parent may still try to justify, rationalize, minimize, or make excuses for her daughter's behaviour. Remember, just as you taught your children, you control only 50 percent of this relationship—you can't make the other parent help her daughter accept responsibility for her bullying behaviours. But the way you handle it will greatly influence her response to you. You are not attacking her child, you are attacking a problem, and you would like to offer her some solutions that worked for you with your children. At the end of the meeting, you will have a better idea of what you will need to do next. Ideally, it will involve giving the girl another opportunity to play at your house. But if there is no resolution, you may have to insist that for a while she will not be able to play in your yard. This is the least desirable outcome, but sometimes it is a necessary one. You can let the parent know that you would like to make this work for everyone and that you will check in at a later date to see if it can be worked out. Often, time and distance will make a difference in the way the parent views the situation and the way the daughter decides to play—especially if other parents approach the bully's parent with the same complaint.

Sometimes, it is helpful if a group of parents express the same concern together and do it in a way that is respectful and assertive. It will help no one if you "gang up" on the bully's parent and launch into a tirade about how awful her child is. But by standing up together, you can help your children be safe and help a bully come around to playing a new, more productive role in the neighbourhood. During the time all of these interactions may take, it is important that you talk with your children about how to stand up for themselves, how to report any dangerous situations—and how to treat even this bully in a respectful way. When we respond with a generous spirit, wisdom, discernment, abundant kindness, and mercy, when we help alleviate the suffering of others and offer them our compassion and empathy, we create caring communities and safe harbours for all of our children.

Rewriting the Script

The bully, the bullied, and the bystander—I hope you now have a clearer understanding of these roles and how the interactions involved in such role-playing, though commonplace in our culture, are not healthy, not normal, certainly not necessary, and in fact are devastating to the children playing them. We as parents and educators can rewrite the script and create for our children alternative, healthier roles that require no pretence and no violence. With care and commitment, we can rechannel the behaviours of the bully into positive leadership activities; acknowledge the nonaggressive behaviours of the bullied child as strengths that can be developed and are honoured; and transform the role of the bystander into that of a witness, someone willing to stand up, speak out, and act against injustice. A daunting task, but a necessary one. When farm workers organizing in the United States faced what appeared to be insurmountable obstacles in their fight for recognition of their dignity and worth as human beings, for decent wages, and for decent living conditions, human rights activist César Chávez challenged them to say "*Sí, se puede*" (Yes, it is possible). Breaking the cycle of violence and creating ever widening circles of caring. Yes, it is possible.

> *Never doubt that a small group of thoughtful, committed citizens can change the world. Indeed, it is the only thing that ever has.*
>
> —Margaret Mead

Sources

Excerpt from the motion picture *The Breakfast Club*. Copyright © 2003 by Universal Studios. Courtesy of Universal Studios Publishing Rights, a Division of Universal Studios Licensing, Inc. All rights reserved. Excerpt from the motion picture *Chocolat*. Reprinted courtesy of Miramax Films.

Excerpt from Harper Lee, *To Kill a Mockingbird*. Reprinted courtesy of HarperCollins*Publishers*. Copyrighted © 1999. Excerpt from Janna Juvonen and Sandra Graham, *Peer Harassment in School*. Reprinted courtesy of Guildford Press. Excerpt from Dr Phillip McGraw, "We're in Crisis," in *O* magazine (June 2001). Reprinted courtesy of the author. *Lost Boys: Why Our Sons Turn Violent and How We Can Save Them* by James Garbarino. Copyright © 1999 by James Garbarino. Reprinted with permission of The Free Press, an imprint of Simon & Schuster Trade Publishing Group. *The Nurture Assumption: Why Children Turn Out the Way They Do* by Judith Rich Harris. Copyright © 1998 by Judith Rich Harris. Reprinted with permission of The Free Press, an imprint of Simon & Schuster Trade Publishing Group. Excerpt from Neil Kurshan, *Raising Your Child to Be a Mensch*. Reprinted with the permission of Scribner, an imprint of Simon & Schuster Adult Publishing Group. Copyright © 1987 Neil Kurshan. Excerpt

Index